"It's Amazing, Isn't It?"

he said finally. "About the statue . . . the resemblance is uncanny."

"What?" Danielle looked up at the statue of the proudly sensuous *Woman,* then back at him, uncomprehendingly.

"You really don't see it, do you?" He smiled. "You could have posed for it." Danielle looked back up at the statue warily.

"If you'd let your hair down, like hers, there's no way you could miss it. And the mouth and eyes are practically identical to yours. As for the body . . ." His amber eyes swept over her, making her feel every bit as naked as the statue. "It's you."

"That's absurd," Danielle snapped. "I'm not anything like . . . that!"

GINA CAIMI

started making up her own fairy tales when she was six years old. It was the only way she could get through arithmetic class. She sculpts as a hobby, adores the opera, ballet and old movies, but writing remains her major passion. And she still hates arithmetic.

Dear Reader:

SILHOUETTE DESIRE is an exciting new line of contemporary romances from Silhouette Books. During the past year, many Silhouette readers have written in telling us what other types of stories they'd like to read from Silhouette, and we've kept these comments and suggestions in mind in developing SILHOUETTE DESIRE.

DESIREs feature all of the elements you like to see in a romance, plus a more sensual, provocative story. So if you want to experience all the excitement, passion and joy of falling in love, then SIL-HOUETTE DESIRE is for you.

Karen Solem
Editor-in-Chief
Silhouette Books

GINA CAIMI
A Wilder Enchantment

Silhouette Desire
Published by Silhouette Books New York
America's Publisher of Contemporary Romance

Silhouette Books by Gina Caimi

Passionate Awakening (DES #125)
A Wilder Enchantment (DES #174)

 SILHOUETTE BOOKS, a Division of Simon & Schuster, Inc.
1230 Avenue of the Americas, New York, N.Y. 10020

Copyright © 1984 by Gina Caimi
Cover artwork copyright © 1984 Doreen Minuto

Distributed by Pocket Books

ISBN: 0-671-52381-3

First Silhouette Books printing November, 1984

10 9 8 7 6 5 4 3 2 1

America's Publisher of Contemporary Romance

Printed in the U.S.A.

BC91

A Wilder
Enchantment

1

The Valmont Art Gallery, an imposing Spanish adobe building, would easily have dominated Dolores Street in Carmel on any occasion. Tonight, with its lights blazing and the almost palpable excitement of an opening spilling out onto the quaint, pine-dotted street, it reigned supreme. Just as César Valmont himself had once reigned over Carmel's unique artists' colony, Danielle thought with a strange mixture of pride and bitterness while she waited impatiently in the office at the back of the gallery for Maggie Carson.

He certainly continued to hold sway in here, she noted wryly. All four walls of the office were covered with photos of Valmont spanning the fifties and sixties, when he was still at his peak as an artist and a celebrity. There were early pictures of Valmont with the other giants of the abstract expressionist movement. There was Valmont indulging various movie stars of the period, Valmont looking progressively bored in the company of Presidents Eisenhower, Kennedy and Johnson, and Valmont and Picasso smiling ferally at each other in a wonderful candid shot taken in Picasso's Paris studio.

There wasn't a single personal photograph in the entire collection, Danielle suddenly realized. Not so much as a snapshot of Valmont with any of his four wives and three legitimate children, let alone one with her. It was as if they had never existed.

Danielle refused to take notice of the long-forgotten feeling starting to knot up her stomach. Instead, with the practiced eye of an efficiency expert, she coolly noted how carefully each photo had been framed and mounted, how perfectly they were lined up and how dramatically the recessed lamps spotlighted them. The total effect was that of a shrine—a shrine dedicated to Valmont, the artist, the genius, the supreme egotist. A shrine that would now become a memorial.

With a harsh sigh, Danielle turned away. But there was no turning away from that dominating presence. It surrounded her. What the hell could be taking Maggie Carson so long? she wondered irritably, feeling as though she were suffocating.

She strode over to the door, pulled it open and drew in a long, ragged breath of air. It reeked of oil paints and varnish. Her fingers tightened around the doorknob as a long-forgotten memory pushed its way into her consciousness.

She was six years old, standing in this same room, on

this very same spot. There was a reason why she'd been allowed into the inner sanctum but she couldn't remember what it was, only the feeling that went with it. They didn't want her here anymore . . . because she didn't belong . . . there was something wrong with her . . .

That same feeling was a solid knot in the pit of her stomach now as Danielle stared hesitantly through the open door at the exclusive-looking crowd milling about the art gallery. The men exuded the kind of nonchalant power only inherited money can buy and the women displayed the elegance and breeding that went with being from the best families.

She suddenly felt totally inadequate. Releasing the doorknob, she stepped back into the office. She couldn't go out there looking like this. Her clothes were all wrong. Besides being too sporty, her white linen suit was terribly wrinkled from hours of driving, and her black silk blouse felt as wilted as she did.

She'd look over the gallery some other time, she decided. After all, her interest was purely business.

A large photo of Valmont caught her eye as she turned to close the door quietly behind her. Something about it, either the arrogant glare of those all-knowing eyes or the cruel slash of his smile, infuriated her. With the same wide, deep-violet eyes, she glared right back at him. He had no power over her anymore. She wasn't that shy, insecure little girl he'd banished from Carmel over twenty years ago along with her mother, the mistress he'd grown tired of. She was a self-sufficient young woman of twenty-nine now and a success in her own field. And, as for not belonging, she had more right to be here than any of those other people because she now owned the place.

It seemed to Danielle that Valmont's smile was one of pure mockery. Turning her back on it, as she'd deliberately turned her back on the art world and everything that went with it years ago, she walked out of the office and slammed the door.

The first thing she was going to do when she took over the gallery, she promised herself, was get rid of all those damn photographs!

Stopping only to pick up a program, along with a complimentary glass of champagne, Danielle continued into the main gallery where the one-man show of sculptures by a certain Devlin Wilder was being held. She still felt terribly self-conscious but was able to feign the interest most people assume in art galleries or museums. She didn't have to pretend for long, for she soon found herself riveted by the unexpected power of the works on display.

She didn't know the first thing about sculpture and she certainly didn't know what to make of these. She wasn't even sure she liked them, but there was no denying their impact. The work was gritty, passionate and totally committed. As Danielle moved from one to another in a kind of daze, she was struck by the incredible physicality of the mostly nude figures. They were so—lush was the only word she could think of. Lush and unashamedly, almost disturbingly, sensual. She felt both attracted and repelled. She couldn't take her eyes off them. It was all she could do not to reach out and touch them.

"The authenticity is quite remarkable," a svelte, elegant brunette declared to her equally stunning blond companion as they stopped in front of the statue that Danielle was admiring.

"I'm just glad bodies are back." The blond laughed throatily, scrutinizing each powerful line and curve of the life-size bronze "Surfer" with bold, pale gray eyes.

"Definitely," the brunette agreed with a world-weary sigh. "I don't know about you, but I've been bored for years with minimalism."

The cool gray glance lingered on the outline of obvious masculinity straining against the swimsuit. "I'll take maximum over minimum any day of the week," she drawled. "Didn't I tell you he was extremely talented?"

"You should know, dear."

Embarrassed by the personal slant the conversation was taking, Danielle turned her attention to her program, but she needn't have bothered. After an initial glance at her travel-wrinkled suit, the two women had dismissed her entirely. She might as well have been another statue standing there.

"I was talking about his talent as a sculptor, darling."

"He's definitely in the avant-garde of the new figuration, I'll give him that much."

Tossing her long, streaked-blond hair, the other woman laughed suggestively again. "Well, I think he's just the greatest, I don't care where he is," she flung over her bare shoulder as she sauntered over to the next statue.

Moving in the opposite direction, Danielle stopped in front of a life-size statue of a nude girl. No, she wasn't nude, Danielle decided on closer inspection, she was naked. No other term could honestly describe her. And she wasn't a girl either; she was very much a woman.

Her strong legs were planted firmly apart, her arms reaching up as if to take the entire sky in their generous embrace. Her back was arched, thrusting her full breasts upward. Her alabaster skin had been polished to warm, glowing life, and the provocative smile on her full lips declared how proud she was of her sensuality. Yet, strangely, there was nothing lewd or suggestive about her.

Eve must have looked like that before she learned of her own nakedness, Danielle thought to her amazement. Once again, she felt attracted and repelled—and a bit envious! It wasn't the statue's lush beauty she envied, since Danielle, who possessed the same full breasts and well-rounded hips, had always longed for the elegant slimness of a Vogue model. Rather, it was the total acceptance of her own sensuality and the joy she seemed to find in being a woman.

With a wistful sigh, Danielle moved from directly in front of the statue to one side in order to view it from another angle. As she turned, she was stopped by an equally stunning sight. She found herself as riveted as she'd been by the sculptures.

The man could easily have been one of those sculptures. He had that same raw, larger-than-life quality. He seemed to be in his late thirties and had to be at least six feet four since he towered over everyone else in the place. There was something vaguely familiar about him and Danielle thought he might be a celebrity of some kind. Certainly, the expression on the upturned faces of the women surrounding him was that of adoring fans.

Taking a long gulp of champagne, she suddenly realized why he seemed familiar. He reminded her of Michelangelo's famous statue of David. The David was one of her favorite works of art; it had always epitomized the ideal of male beauty to her. She had never expected to see such beauty in a living man.

He had the same powerful shoulders and back, the same natural grace. The jacket of the conservative pinstripe suit he wore hugged the wide expanse of chest before tapering down a surprisingly narrow waist and lean hips. The well-cut trousers outlined long, muscular legs.

He even had the same large, out-of-proportion hands as David, she noticed, when he took a long, lusty swig of champagne. His fingers were wide, with bluntly cut nails and there was a blood blister on his thumb. His were not the typical affluent businessman's hands. They were hands that built things. Or tore them apart. She wondered which. She wondered how they would feel on her skin. . . .

As if he'd heard her shocking thought, the man suddenly turned and looked straight at her. His deep-set eyes widened in surprise and he seemed to stop breathing for a moment, as if he recognized her but was amazed at her being there. His vibrant gaze left her face to move over every curve of her body. But it wasn't the look Danielle usually got from men and which she'd resigned herself to years ago, the kind that undressed her while trying to guess at the body beneath the clothes. His look was one of recognition—as if he knew exactly how she looked naked and was merely confirming it. Somehow it was even worse because she had no defense against the strange intimacy of it.

She stepped back in front of the statue, effectively cutting the man off from view again, but he'd already started toward her impulsively, leaving one of his female admirers in the middle of a sentence. Before Danielle could decide what to do, he'd covered the short distance between them.

"I don't believe it," he murmured in a deeply resonant, somewhat scratchy voice that fit him perfectly. "I really don't believe this." His tone implied that he knew her.

She felt oddly disappointed that he would use such an obvious line. "No, we've never met before."

"I know," he admitted softly. "If we had, I would have remembered." Yet he continued staring at her as though he knew her, searching her face with a kind of baffled wonder.

He was even more devastating close up—warm and golden with his deep tan, his tawny, sun-streaked hair and amber eyes. He wasn't conventionally handsome but had a strong, arresting face. It was a face that refused to be ignored, all sharp, uncompromising lines, except for his mouth, which was surprisingly soft, sensitive—too soft, too sensitive for a man, she decided. It was the most beautiful mouth she'd ever seen.

It turned up at the corners; he was obviously aware of and pleased with her appraisal. Danielle suddenly realized that she'd been staring, but she couldn't look away. He seemed to be having the same problem. She thought this kind of thing happened only in the movies.

"It's amazing, isn't it?" he said finally, making her wonder if he were also aware of her trembling hands and the butterflies in her stomach. "About the statue . . . the resemblance is uncanny."

"What?" Danielle looked up at the statue of the proudly sensuous "Woman," then back at him, uncomprehendingly.

"You really don't see it, do you?" He smiled wryly. "You could have posed for it."

"Oh, come on now," Danielle scoffed. But at least this line was more original than the first.

"Just look at her," he insisted. His frown of annoyance at her refusal to believe him seemed genuine enough. Danielle looked back up at the statue warily.

"Your hair is black and you've got it pulled tight into that . . . chignon or whatever it's called," he muttered disapprovingly, "but if you'd let your hair down, like hers, there's no way you could miss it. Here, look at the full lips and those big doe eyes." He reached up to trace the outline of the mouth and eyes in the air with surprising delicacy. "They're practically identical to yours."

Tilting his head back, he squinted first at her face, then at the statue's. "OK, your nose is finer . . . and your bone structure isn't quite as strong as hers, but it's not off by much. As for the body . . ." His amber eyes swept over her full curves with the same intimate knowledge as before, making her feel every bit as naked as the statue. "It's you."

"That's absurd," Danielle snapped. She felt totally vulnerable and furious at him for making her feel that way. "I'm not anything like . . . that!"

"Are you sure?" he asked thoughtfully, as though they were discussing a subject about which he was infinitely more knowledgeable. "In spite of your deliberately proper, almost austere facade, I get the feeling you're *exactly* like her . . . under the skin."

Before Danielle could come up with an appropriately scathing reply, they were interrupted by a dapper, middle-aged man who wore his evening clothes as if they were a second skin. "There you are, Devlin. Great show, old man. Your best work yet."

Danielle gasped soundlessly and glared at Devlin Wilder as if he'd deliberately misrepresented himself. He certainly didn't look anything like an artist, not with that conservative suit and carefully groomed appearance. Then she remembered those hands.

"Thanks, Lyle," he said warmly.

Damn it, she thought, why did he have to be an artist? It wasn't fair. There should be a law requiring all artists to wear a sign around their necks: Beware— Artist. Approach at your own risk.

The suave British-accented voice interrupted her absurd thoughts. "Devlin, aren't you going to introduce me to this lovely creature?"

"No, Lyle."

The older man ignored him to turn his considerable charm on Danielle. "I'm sorry to interrupt, my dear, but I've been watching you from across the room and I just had to meet you." He extended a lean, manicured hand. From the look of it, the hardest work it had ever done was lift a martini glass. "I'm Lyle Sheldon."

"Danielle Adams," she replied automatically, giving

her hand politely in return, thanks to years of careful training at Miss Bowers' Academy for Young Ladies.

"Enchanté." Instead of shaking her hand, he bent his sleek, steel-gray head over it and kissed it in the continental manner. Devlin shot him a murderous look. "I can see now why Devlin insists on keeping you all to himself. You're even lovelier in . . . the flesh, shall we say?"

"Excuse me?"

Lyle Sheldon turned his frankly admiring gaze on the statue by way of explanation as Devlin threw his head back and roared with laughter.

"Uh, Mr. Sheldon, you're . . ."

"Lyle, I insist."

"You're mistaken. I never posed for that statue."

"Oh, my dear, you musn't be ashamed," he chided. "It's simply exquisite . . . and so are you."

"But I'm not ashamed . . . I haven't done anything to be ashamed of!" she protested so heatedly that it sounded phony even to her. "Mr. Wilder, will you . . ."

"Dev, darling, here you are!" The throaty exclamation, which interrupted Danielle's plea, announced the return of the blond she'd seen earlier. Remembering the conversation she'd overheard, Danielle found herself studying the woman with intense curiosity.

She appeared to be in her mid-forties but was easily one of the most attractive women present. From the top of her professionally streaked and coiffed hair to the painted tips of her toes, she was a carefully crafted work of art. The masklike perfection of her face could have been created only by a master makeup artist. The designer gown which draped her tall, lithe body in a fluid column of aquamarine chiffon was also created by a master. But the artistry in her seductive smile and walk, that throaty drawl of a voice, was all her own.

"If you only knew what I've been through for you, Dev Wilder," she murmured provocatively, "dragging that bore of a May Warren around for the last hour. But I just know she's going to buy and when she does I insist on a commission." She flashed him a smile that was an almost desperate attempt at girlishness before turning to Lyle Sheldon as a kind of afterthought. "Lyle, pet, how are you enjoying the show?"

"Smashing. Simply smashing," he purred at Danielle. "My dear, I'd like you to meet Danielle Adams. Danielle . . . my wife, Valerie."

Thanks once again to Miss Bowers' rigorous training, Danielle managed to conceal her shock. Reminding herself that this kind of sophisticated immorality was typical of artists and that her set of values didn't apply here, she nodded politely. "Mrs. Sheldon."

Valerie Sheldon's smile lost some of its brilliance as she looked intently at Danielle. "I thought you said you didn't use a model for this statue, Dev," she accused lightly.

"Oh, my God," Danielle muttered in disbelief. Was the resemblance really that obvious? Did everyone else in the place assume she'd posed like that? She felt totally exposed. She could have strangled Devlin Wilder with her bare hands just to wipe the smug grin off his face.

He shrugged those massive shoulders. "I told you" was all he said. He obviously had no intention of clearing up the misunderstanding since he was too busy enjoying himself at her expense.

"I did not pose for that statue!" Danielle exploded in sheer frustration. "Nothing on this earth could get me to pose like . . . that!"

Husband and wife exchanged knowing looks. They obviously didn't believe her, nor could they understand what she was making such a fuss about. Danielle couldn't understand it either. She'd always prided herself on being able to handle the most complex situations; her job demanded it. She knew she was overreacting, but there was nothing she could do about it. She turned on Devlin Wilder with an ice-cold fury. "Will you stop this? Will you tell them I never posed for you?"

His teasing grin changed into a perplexed frown as he finally realized how upset she was. "Miss Adams is right . . . believe it or not," he admitted at last. "She didn't pose for the statue. There was no model."

"But you always work from life," Valerie Sheldon insisted, clearly unconvinced.

"No, not always. Sometimes I work from memory or . . ."

"That must have been *quite* a memory," Lyle Sheldon interrupted with a suggestive smirk. The stricken look on Danielle's face rivaled that of his wife.

Strangely enough, even the sculptor seemed put off by his innuendo. "Not *quite*, Lyle, since we only met a few minutes ago," he replied coolly. "The statue was pure fantasy on my part."

"How extraordinary!" Valerie Sheldon laughed, but her laughter had an edge to it, an undercurrent of jealous anger. If her husband was aware of it, that awareness didn't show on his lean, elegant features. "It must be some kick to meet your . . . fantasy woman in real life," she added sarcastically.

"Yes, it is," Devlin admitted to Danielle with a devastatingly sensuous smile. The message in that smile and in those intense amber eyes was every bit as raw and compelling as his work, and Danielle was as helplessly riveted by it.

"Well, well, this show is turning into a genuine happening," Lyle Sheldon declared with undisguised glee.

Danielle was grateful for his interruption this time, even though it was suggestive, because it snapped her out of the absurd daze she was in. She turned to him with a forced smile. "I'm sorry I can't stay for the finish. Nice meeting you all."

Turning abruptly on her heels, she was about to walk away when a huge hand grabbed hers from behind, restraining her. She didn't have to look to know whose hand it was. She'd known that this was how it would feel. What she hadn't counted on was the effect it would have on her.

"Come on," Devlin ordered softly, his raspy voice exerting the same subtle pressure on her as his hand. "We'll see you both later," he muttered vaguely at the Sheldons. The surprised look on Valerie Sheldon's face mirrored Danielle's.

"Hey, wait a minute," she protested as she found herself being pulled along by him. He chose to ignore her as he concentrated on wending his way through the crowd.

The crowd had settled into tight little circles, each one a droning beehive of intense intellectual argument. At his approach, arguments were dropped, to be picked up only after he'd passed. Danielle couldn't help noticing how people moved automatically out of his way, as though a force of nature were coming through, or the way he was being stared at by men and women alike. He seemed oblivious to the effect he was having, but Danielle was cringing inside as she now found herself being included in those fascinated stares.

Struggling to regain control of herself and the situation, she sought to free her hand from the strong, warm crush of his without being obvious about it. If there was anything she hated, it was creating a scene in public. She felt sure that he knew this somehow, was depending on it, and it made her even angrier. "Just what do you think you're doing?" she muttered between clenched teeth, twisting her wrist again.

He tightened his hold on her. His hand was so large that it easily swallowed up hers, so warm that it sent cold shivers up her arm. "You didn't really think I'd let you get away from me that easily, did you?" The tone of his voice was as unnervingly intimate as his smile yet held a trace of humor. "It's not every day one of my statues comes to life."

He tugged on her hand suddenly, pulling her close to him. She was about to protest again when she saw that she was about to bump into a couple she hadn't realized were coming toward them. Caught off-balance, she bumped into him instead. The side of her breast brushed against his muscular arm, and she inhaled a whiff of musky after-shave mingling with the tangy male scent of him. She was suddenly grateful that his hand was there to steady her and even more relieved that he hadn't noticed her reaction.

He was too busy scanning the rest of the gallery. "There must be someplace in this madhouse where we can go to be alone and talk," he muttered impatiently. "I know . . . there's an office at the back of the . . ."

"No!" Danielle stopped dead, refusing to take another step. She didn't care about making a scene anymore. She'd had all she could take. She pulled her hand away angrily, shoving it into her jacket pocket. "No, this is as far as I go. Besides . . ."—as he'd just reminded her—"I'm meeting someone here."

"You . . . are?"

"That's right," she said coldly, turning away. It bothered her that she had to look away from him in order to get back her usual composure. She began searching through the crowd, but even with her back to him, she could feel the power of his presence. The intensity of his gaze was like a laser beam burning clear through her.

"Oh, there she is." Danielle sighed with relief when she spotted Maggie Carson's assistant, who was searching frantically for her from the hallway leading to the office.

"Is *that* who you're meeting . . . Ellen?" he asked. The statement was accompanied by an expulsion of breath that brushed the nape of her neck, sending a tiny shiver all the way down her spine.

Danielle started waving to Ellen like someone marooned on a desert island who's just sighted a rescue ship on the horizon. Just as the girl was acknowledging her, Devlin stepped in front of Danielle, forcing her to look up at him again. He was so close that she couldn't see anything but him. Damned if he wasn't the most impossibly attractive man she'd ever met.

"I have to go," she insisted a bit too forcefully. "I'm here on very important business." She couldn't help wondering who she was trying to convince, him or herself. From the wry look on his face, he seemed to be wondering the same thing.

"I have to go now," she repeated, indicating with the empty champagne glass she'd been clutching like a life preserver, that he was blocking her way.

"All right," he agreed amiably, without moving a step. "But you'll come back after . . . when you're through, and we'll go someplace where we can talk, OK?" It was more of an appeal than a question.

If Danielle hadn't known better, she could easily have been taken in by that surprisingly tentative smile, the soft pleading in his eyes. But she knew better.

"I'm sure it'll be too late by then," she said, taking several halting steps to one side in an effort to get around him.

With one sure, long-legged stride he was in front of her again. "I don't care how late you'll be. I'll wait."

With a certainty she couldn't understand, Danielle knew that Devlin Wilder wasn't a man who would take no for an answer, and since he was an artist, she shuddered to think what crazy stunt he might pull.

"All right," she lied, "but it'll take a couple of hours."

"No problem!" He laughed, a low, sexy rumble of a

laugh. "I've waited for you this long, what's another couple of hours?"

Valerie Sheldon was right, Danielle thought ruefully as she made her way over to where Ellen was waiting for her. Devlin Wilder was an extremely talented man. And sculpture was only one of his talents.

2

Hey, I'm sorry I kept you waiting so long," Ellen said dramatically, emphasizing every other word with the life-or-death intensity of a teenager.

The tiny lines under her eyes and edging the corners of her wide mouth put her in her late twenties, but her tomboyish face and figure made her appear years younger. So did her outfit, which had been put together from various secondhand shops specializing in antique clothes. Indian jewelry dangled from her neck and ears and circled both wrists. Her light brown hair formed a frizzy halo around her head. She reminded Danielle of a leftover flower child.

"I had to drive all the way to Maggie's house and back!" The sheer torture of it was expressed by a tragic sigh as Ellen closed the office door behind her.

"You shouldn't have gone to all that trouble,"

Danielle murmured apologetically. "I could have stayed over one more day if I had to."

"Hey, no trouble." She shrugged good-naturedly, sailing over to the desk. "Besides, I thought I could talk Maggie into coming back here with me. I mean, I can't handle this crowd all by myself." Her collection of silver and turquoise bracelets jangled as she waved Danielle over to the leather chair in front of the desk. "I don't think she'll be up by tomorrow anyway."

"What's wrong?" Danielle hesitated as she was about to sit down. "Is she sick?"

"You know, I'm only supposed to work here after classes and on weekends," Ellen protested. "I'm still going to art school." Pulling the top drawer of the desk open, she began to go through it, adding wistfully, "One of these days *my* paintings will hang here in the gallery."

"I'm sure they will but . . . is Ms. Carson sick?"

"She's been like this ever since Valmont passed away." Shaking her frizzy halo, Ellen sighed dramatically again. "She was his first wife, you know."

"Yes, I . . . I heard." Danielle sank into the chair stiffly. Maggie Carson was the model Valmont had left her mother for.

"You know what people around here say?" Ellen bent over the desk, lowering her voice to a confidential whisper even though they were the only two people in the office. "It went on even after they got divorced . . . every time Valmont came back to Carmel. It was one of those on-again, off-again things. Really heavy, you know, like an old Bette Davis movie!"

Danielle stared into the empty champagne glass

she'd brought into the office because she'd been too flustered by her encounter with Devlin Wilder to remember to put it down. "Did she leave any keys for me?"

"Oh, sure. That's what I'm looking for. They're supposed to be here in the desk somewhere." She went back to rummaging through the top drawer. "So anyway, when she got the telegram, it really hit her hard."

"I'm sorry," Danielle said sincerely. She'd never blamed Maggie Carson. Knowing Valmont, if it hadn't been her, it would have been someone else. "Has she seen a doctor?"

"She was coming out of it OK. She got very involved setting up Dev Wilder's show but then . . ." She paused in her muddled search for the keys to look across the desk at Danielle. "I saw you talking to Dev when I came in . . ." Her hazel eyes took on the worship-glazed look of a rock star groupie. "He sure is a hunk, isn't he?"

"He is rather . . . attractive," Danielle allowed, twirling the champagne glass with suddenly nervous fingers.

"He can give me anatomy lessons any time!" Ellen gushed.

"I'm sure he'd be glad to oblige, but from what I've seen you may have to wait in line." Danielle was surprised by the jealous edge in her tone. She put the champagne glass down on top of the desk. "You were saying . . . about Ms. Carson?"

"Oh, yeah. So then, last Friday she went into this deep funk again. Out of nowhere." Ellen shrugged uncomprehendingly and began rifling through the center drawer.

"Last . . . Friday?" Danielle murmured thoughtfully. That was the day she'd called Maggie Carson long-distance to tell her why she was coming to Carmel. She was sure that Valmont's ex-wife had expected him to leave the art gallery to her since she'd been running it for twenty years.

"Hey, here it is!" Ellen's high-pitched squeal of excitement brought Danielle back to the present. "These are the keys to Valmont's studio and directions on how to get there." She handed Danielle the sealed envelope with her name written on it. "Are you an artist too?"

"No, thank God!" Danielle laughed bitterly. She noticed that Ellen's eyes were practically feverish with curiosity but she wasn't about to explain her illegitimate relationship to Valmont. She knew exactly what her reaction would be: really heavy, just like an old Bette Davis movie!

"Please tell Ms. Carson I'll call her as soon as I get settled." Pocketing the envelope, Danielle got to her feet. "And thanks for going to all this trouble, Ellen. I really appreciate it."

"Hey, no trouble." Ellen broke into a wide, friendly grin. "Taking care of that mob out there, that's going to be trouble."

"Is this the type of clientele you usually get?" Danielle asked, preceding her to the door.

"No way. This is a strictly San Francisco crowd. Mrs. Sheldon and her friends came down especially for Dev Wilder's opening." Just mentioning the sculptor made her eyes go glazy again. "That's where he's from originally, you know, very high society."

Danielle hesitated in the doorway as she remembered her promise to Devlin to meet him when she was free. It was a promise she had no intention of keeping. But she'd have to find a way of leaving without his noticing.

She couldn't help smiling at her own naivete. He was sure to have forgotten her promise and her by now and was probably working his charms on some other, more receptive female. He might already have left with his new choice. He certainly seemed hungry for a woman's company. That thought irritated Danielle but she shrugged it off. If he *was* still there, he'd be too lost in his crowd of admirers to notice her anyway, she assured herself, as she continued resolutely out the door.

She spotted him instantly. There was no way she could have missed him. He'd stationed himself at the end of the hall where she'd be forced to pass him to get back into the gallery. She managed to suppress a tiny thrill of satisfaction and concentrate on her determination to have nothing more to do with him. Since he was standing in profile, surrounded by the usual adoring fans, Danielle was certain that she'd be able to get away without his noticing her.

Indicating the back entrance of the gallery, which opened onto the parking lot, she whispered over her shoulder to Ellen, "I think I'll go out the way I came in."

"Hey, you're not leaving already?" Ellen's high-pitched squeal of protest reverberated throughout the hall. It went through Danielle like the shriek of a siren and she bolted for the back door. Out of the corner of her eye, she caught a blurred glimpse of Devlin Wilder's face as he turned toward her. She was positive she'd managed to get outside before he saw her.

She tugged at the heavy metal door behind her, trying to get it to close faster, but succeeded only in getting it to move in fits and starts, its air hinges wheezing an asthmatic protest. Then, as if it had a will of its own, it jerked the doorknob out of her hand and reopened, to reveal a scowling Devlin Wilder.

He stared at her silently for a moment before walking through the door, while Danielle struggled to find an appropriate excuse for her behavior. She felt like a fool for having agreed to see him and wondered how she was going to get out of it without making an even bigger fool of herself. She couldn't blame him for being angry with her—nobody liked being stood up.

"So, where would you like to go?" he asked amiably, as if this were exactly how and where they'd planned to meet. His reaction was so unexpected that it left her speechless, but he didn't bother to wait for her answer anyway. "There's a great little pub just a couple of blocks from here, OK?"

"No!" Danielle recovered her composure quickly, knowing she would certainly end up in that pub if she didn't. "Sorry, but it's too late and I'm very tired."

"Just one drink," he insisted lightly. "You do owe me, you know."

"Really?" She certainly had to give him credit for gall. "How do you figure that?"

"I'm sure you didn't exist until I dreamed you up. The least you can do is have a drink with me." A disarmingly self-mocking smile tugged at the corners of his mouth.

Danielle was forced to admit that if he wasn't an artist, she'd have gone just about anywhere with him. But he was an artist. And sedutive charm, she reminded herself bitterly, was as much an artist's stock-in-trade as oil paints or alabaster.

"Some other time," she lied. Two lies in the space of an hour. Not bad for someone who'd always prided herself on being scrupulously honest. This man was already bringing out the worst in her, she thought ruefully, as she stepped off the narrow landing onto the stairs leading down to the parking lot.

"Careful," he warned, reaching out to grab her arm.

Danielle stiffened automatically. She wasn't used to having a total stranger take her arm as though they'd been friends for years—something he was making a habit of—and it irritated her, almost as much as her reaction to his unnerving touch. "Look, I can walk and chew gum at the same time!"

"I don't doubt it," he said wryly, continuing to hold her in a casual but firm grip. "But it gets pretty tricky down here . . . in the dark."

"I'll bet," she muttered under her breath. If he heard her, he chose to ignore her sarcasm and concentrate on their descent.

Before they got halfway down the stairs, Danielle realized that Devlin was right. The wooden steps *were* steep, a couple of them dangerously wobbly. There was no bannister and the single bulb over the doorway provided barely adequate illumination. Still, she couldn't help thinking that he was taking advantage of the situation. Did he really have to hold onto her so possessively, keeping her slightly off-balance so that she was forced to lean against him for support? The awareness of his strong, hard body rubbing against hers as they moved in unison left her shakier than the wobbly steps ever could. Yet the look he slanted her seemed innocent of any ulterior motive.

"Watch out for that last step," he murmured thickly, making Danielle wonder if he was as indifferent as he looked. The step groaned under their combined weight as it threatened to cave in at the middle, causing the whole side of her body to press even tighter against the length of his. Something like an electric shock went through her. She was sure that he felt it because his body stiffened.

The instant they touched solid ground, she pulled away from him and he released his powerful grip. But his broad hand glided slowly down her arm, sandpapery fingers lingering on hers for a moment as if reluctant to let go.

Danielle couldn't understand how this man could have such an effect on her. Probably because no man ever had. She was sure it was just nerves. She'd been overreacting all evening. Coming back here had obviously upset her more than she'd anticipated. The sooner she got away from him . . . from here, the better off she'd be.

"Where's your car?" Devlin asked matter-of-factly before Danielle had a chance to say good night. "I'd better drive you. As I'm sure you've noticed, there aren't many signs in Carmel. Unless you're familiar with the place, it's very easy to get lost . . . especially at night."

"I can find my own way," she assured him firmly

even though she was having trouble finding her car. She wondered vaguely how he knew that she wasn't a native.

"If you'd rather, then tell me where you're going," he insisted politely, "and I'll drive on ahead in my car. You can follow in yours."

Danielle was almost tempted to take him up on his offer because the unusual lack of signs and house numbers had been a problem earlier. She decided that getting lost in a strange town in the middle of the night was less dangerous than driving back to her motel with him.

"That won't be necessary," she said coolly while she continued to search for her car, trying not to look as disoriented as she felt. When she'd parked earlier, it was still daylight and there hadn't been as many cars.

Even the parking lots here were artistic, she noted wryly. The kind of parking lot she was accustomed to back home was a concrete square or rectangle, with neatly defined spaces, marked off by precise white lines that left no doubt as to how or where to park. This parking lot sprawled unevenly among a mini-forest of Monterey pines, and cars were parked every which way. Nothing had been done to pave or level off the ground or to remove the gnarled trees from where they stood and several of them stood smack in the middle of the lot, forcing the cars to park around them.

To add to the confusion, instead of the bright-as-day lights of normal parking lots, the only illumination came from the tiny light bulbs dotting the length of each pine like Christmas tree decorations. It was all very lovely, an earthly reflection of the myriad stars dotting the sky overhead—but not much use in trying to locate a car in the dark. The moon wasn't much help either. It was a pale, delicate sliver, circled by a hazy glow. A very romantic setting, Danielle was forced to admit, if you were into romantic parking lots.

Surprisingly, her eyes became accustomed to the offbeat lighting and she was soon able to make out the outline of her car. She was also acutely aware of Devlin Wilder's presence as he continued to hover silently by her side. There was something unnerving about his patient silence. It implied an easy acceptance of their being together, a friendly intimacy.

Starting resolutely toward her car, Danielle tossed a quick, final good night at him.

He didn't catch it. "Do you like seafood?" he asked pleasantly, falling right into step with her.

"What?"

"You know . . ." He grinned wryly. "Prawns, abalone, Dungeness crabs. Seafood."

The look she slanted him assured him that she knew what seafood was.

"Do you?"

"Well . . . yes," she admitted because she couldn't think of anything else to say.

"Great." His grin widened into a disarming smile. "Then I've got just the place for dinner."

"Look, I told you. It's late and I'm tired."

"Not tonight," he agreed reasonably. "I'm letting you off the hook this time. I meant dinner tomorrow night."

"I'm busy tomorrow night," Danielle lied, stepping up her pace.

He quickened his pace to match hers and they continued wending their way around the creatively parked cars, pine needles crackling underfoot. The fresh scent of pine floated on a soft breeze, mingling with the fine mist that suffused the air and smelled of the sea. "Monday then."

"No, it's . . . impossible." Why didn't she just tell him that she didn't want to go out with him? She'd never had any trouble dealing with a man's unwanted attentions before. She was beginning to wonder whether Devlin Wilder's attentions were as unwelcome as she'd like to believe.

Stopping in front of her car, Danielle let out a small sigh of frustration. If only he weren't so charming and gentlemanly. If only he weren't an artist!

"OK, when?" he asked evenly, insistence softly edging his tone as he halted by the front fender.

Danielle began digging around in her shoulder bag for her car keys. "This is going to be a very hectic week for me. I'm moving into my new place and . . ."

"Then you're not just passing through?" he blurted out, sounding oddly relieved. "I assumed you were here on vacation."

Danielle paused in her search for the keys to look over at him defensively. "Why do you say that?" Was it that obvious that she didn't belong?

"Well, you're obviously not from around here."

"How do you know?"

"Just little things. Your skin is too white. Your clothes are too tailored, and . . . that car." He chuckled warmly as he eyed the dark blue Chevy again. Her large, squarely built car stuck out among the sleek sports cars filling the lot like a bull elephant in a herd of gazelles. "I'd guess you're from . . . the East Coast? New England or . . ."

"That's right," she admitted coolly, resuming her search for the keys. "Boston."

"Welcome to sunny, laid-back California." He seemed happy all of a sudden. He propped himself up against the front fender of her car, his long, muscular legs stretched out comfortably in front of him as if he could afford to relax now. "Are you staying here in Carmel?" he asked matter-of-factly.

"No, I'm staying in . . ." Danielle caught herself just in time as she realized that he was subtly pumping her for information. "In the area. But I'll be spending time here in Carmel." There was no point in trying to hide that fact from him. Since she'd be spending a lot of time at the art gallery, there was no way she could avoid him—professionally.

"If you need any help moving in," he offered, "I'd be glad to . . ."

"No, thanks. I can manage," she assured him. If only she could manage to find her car keys. She always kept them in a special compartment but they must have fallen out, gotten buried under the travel things she'd overstuffed her bag with.

"Moving can be quite a hassle," he insisted, watching her increasingly frantic efforts to find her keys with wry amusement. "Especially if you're alone."

Danielle slanted him another defensive look. "What makes you think I'm alone?"

"I can see you're not married. You're not wearing a wedding ring . . . or an engagement ring so . . ." The shadow of a doubt suddenly darkened the light gold of his eyes, grated in his already scratchy voice. "Is there . . . someone else?"

"That's none of your business!"

"I didn't think there was." He shrugged but a smile of relief lit up his impossibly attractive face.

"Well, you're wrong." The fact that Howard was back in Boston and that she'd just broken off their engagement—postponed her decision until the end of the summer, she reminded herself—was beside the point. "There is someone else. His name is Howard Cabot, and we're announcing our engagement in September."

She was glad to see that blinding smile of his fade, but the naked intensity of his gaze as it searched her face for the truth was even more disturbing.

Danielle turned her attention back to locating her keys, digging down to the very bottom of her bag, threatening to spill its contents. She could still feel those piercing eyes studying her every move, trying to penetrate her self-assured pose. She sighed audibly when her hand found, then retrieved the metal key ring.

Devlin eased himself off the fender. "Even if there is someone else," he shrugged as he moved closer to her, "he can't be very important . . . or he's not the right man for you."

"Really?" Danielle laughed at the sheer unmitigated gall of the man. "And how did you figure that one out? *That's* not on the license plate."

"No," he admitted simply. "That's in your eyes."

"My eyes?" she scoffed lightly, determined to keep up her bantering defense. "What's wrong with my eyes?" She concentrated on finding the right key. "Are they too tailored?"

"Oh, no. They're very beautiful. But they're not the eyes of a woman who believes she's loved," he murmured. "They're the saddest eyes I've ever seen. Almost . . . haunted."

Danielle looked at him, violet eyes wide with shock, dark with buried pain. She felt as if he could see right through her, stripping away the protective layers she'd learned to wrap around herself, leaving her totally defenseless.

"Exhausted is . . . what they are." She'd meant the words to come out dripping with sarcasm but her voice cracked. At least she managed to turn away from him with some degree of pride. "I've been on the road since seven this morning," she added, attempting to explain away the cracking of her voice, the trembling of her hand as it fumbled the key into the lock. "I have to go now."

"Why won't you see me again?" Devlin demanded, a new intent in his voice.

Danielle pulled the car door open impatiently. "I've already told you."

"No!" His huge hand came from out of nowhere to slam the door shut again and jerk the key out of the lock. "That's not the real reason."

Danielle spun around to face him. "Give me back my keys."

"Tell me the truth first." His hand balled up into a fist, easily swallowing her entire set of keys—her *only* set of keys. "I know you were attracted to me too . . . the instant we met. I felt it. Then something happened. You deliberately turned it off." He was standing directly in front of her. There was barely enough room for two people of average size between her Chevy and the Porsche parked next to it, and he was far from average. He took up most of the space and towered over her, his thigh grazing hers. "Was it something I said . . . or did?"

"I am not attracted to you," Danielle lied coolly, pulling back from the softly insistent pressure of his thigh. Since there was so little room, she ended up with the small of her back smack up against the hard metal door handle. But she refused to budge from the spot—to do so would be to admit that he did have an effect on her. "But even if I were, I'd never get involved with anyone like you," she blurted out, then kicked herself mentally. He wasn't asking her to get involved with him; a one-night stand was all that he had in mind. "I just don't care for your life-style," she finished haughtily.

"But what do you know about my life-style, or about me?" he persisted, eliminating the bare inch or so of space she'd managed to put between them. "Do you always prejudge people?" He was so close to her that she found it difficult to breathe.

"Will you give me my keys?" she insisted, a thread of hysteria in her voice. He clearly had no intention of doing so, or of moving. Danielle began inching sideways along the car to get past him.

Instantly aware of her intention, Devlin slammed both hands down on the roof of her car, one on each side of her shoulders, effectively holding her captive.

"Just answer me one question, OK?" The tone of his

voice was meant to reassure her that she was in no real danger. Danielle suddenly realized that it had never occurred to her to be afraid of him. She felt sure that he was not the kind of man who would hurt her. At least not physically.

He leaned in on her, his powerful body so close that she could feel the heat emanating from it. He bent his craggy head down to hers as though eager to hear her answer. "Why did you agree to go out with me when you obviously never intended to?" he asked softly, his breath caressing her lips.

"What choice did you give me?" she exploded, shaking as much from her reaction to him as from anger. "You refused to take no for an answer . . . just as you're doing now! What else could I do?"

"You're right." Devlin broke into a self-mocking grin, throwing her completely again. His hands dropped to his sides, releasing her, but not her keys. "Believe it or not, I'm not usually this pushy." He looked genuinely embarrassed by his behavior. "But then this isn't your usual situation."

Still unnerved by this unpredictable, impossible man, Danielle snapped contemptuously, "Isn't it?"

"No, it's not! I wouldn't be standing here making a damn fool of myself if it were!" he shot back at her with more hurt than anger. "This isn't a pickup!"

Danielle stuck her hand out forcefully but she had to concentrate to keep it from shaking. "Can I have my keys now?"

"Is that what you think this is . . . just another pick-up? But you saw the statue, dammit!" He stalked away from her abruptly, brushing her hand out of the way as he did. He stopped just past the trunk of her car, somehow unable to go any farther.

Danielle forgot about her keys. As if mesmerized, she watched in the tense silence while he fought to get himself under control. She didn't believe that even he could fake such a surprising depth of emotion, but she was at a loss to understand it. She decided that he must be a bit crazy. All artists were.

"Valerie Sheldon was right, you know," he said finally to the keys while fingering them one by one. The very act of touching seemed to have a soothing effect on him. But the sensuous way that he was stroking them was having an oddly unsettling effect on Danielle. "That statue *is* my fantasy woman. She's everything I find wondrous and desirable . . . everything I've ever wanted in a woman and never found . . ." He paused and smiled self-consciously. "Until tonight."

He looked over at her then. Even in the semidarkness his eyes were golden, picking up and reflecting the light, glowing with a longing that stirred unwanted feelings deep inside her.

"That's . . . crazy!" she cried in self-defense.

"Why is that crazy?" he demanded, stalking back over to her. "Incredible maybe . . . but why crazy?" He was by her side again, overwhelming her by his sheer presence as he searched her face intently. "Didn't you ever dream of meeting someone who would be everything you wanted to love?"

"Yes . . . of course," she was forced to admit, "but . . ."

"Or is it that you don't believe that *you* could inspire such feelings?" He moved in on her. "Is that why you dress that way and wear your hair like that?"

"If you don't give me my keys this minute," Danielle warned, "I'll . . ." She moved to grab them out of his hand but he was too fast for her.

He buried her keys in his pants pocket, knowing that she wouldn't dare go after them. "That's it, isn't it?" he insisted, but his tone was hushed with surprise. "You're not trying to be coy. You really don't know how lovely you are. How very . . . very . . ."

He seemed to be having trouble finding the right word. He sighed impatiently, and out of frustration or some compelling need to show her in the only way he knew how, he reached out to trace the outline of her face. His touch threw Danielle completely. She felt as though she'd just turned into one of his statues. A sandpapery thumb grazed her startled lips just before his breath did. "Seductive," he rasped, crushing the word softly on her mouth with his.

Normally, Danielle wouldn't have had any trouble handling a simple pass, not even one as unexpected as this. But nothing in her experience had prepared her for the aching tenderness of that kiss, the extraordinary sensitivity of those big hands now hugging her face.

Devlin looked as amazed at his own impulsiveness as Danielle did when he dragged his mouth away from hers. He actually seemed on the verge of apologizing until he saw the dazed glow in Danielle's eyes, her trembling lips. When his mouth took hers this time, he knew exactly what he was doing.

Danielle tried to pull away but he wrapped his

powerful arms around her, drawing her to him, surrounding her while his mouth swallowed up the protest she'd started to utter. His lips were unbelievably soft and warm, his body thrillingly taut with longing. Her own body arched involuntarily into his, sending a shudder through him that reverberated deep inside her.

She never meant to let the kiss go on so long, even though it was the most sensuous kiss she'd ever known, or to open her lips to the softly insistent urging of his tongue, but she did.

The tip of his tongue glided irresistibly over her lips before tracing their inner softness and slowly easing its way inside. The sweet hesitancy of his actions lulled any fears she might have had. Too late she realized that he meant to slowly savor every inch of her mouth. By then he was deep inside, exploring with an intimacy that left her shaking. And all Danielle could do was cling to him with the hands she'd pressed against his sides to push him away.

He groaned with pleasure when he felt her melt against him and drew her even closer against the length of his strong, hard body. His kiss became more intense, opening her up to sensations she never knew existed, to feelings she'd never been capable of. She'd been kissed before, expertly, even passionately, but never with such emotional intensity, with a longing that seemed more than physical. Danielle realized that she was being drawn irrevocably beyond her depth, that now was the time to stop, but she found herself returning his kiss with a hunger that amazed her.

"I knew you'd be like this," he murmured raggedly when he tore his mouth away from hers because they were both out of breath. He cupped her face again as he smiled down into her still dazed eyes with wry humor. "Didn't I tell you that you were just like my 'Woman' . . . under the skin?"

If he'd suddenly thrown a bucket of ice water in her face, he couldn't have shocked her back to reality so completely.

"No, I'm not!" Danielle pushed away from him with such force that her back slammed up against the door of her car and Devlin fell back against the Porsche. "And I'm not like . . . this either!" she cried angrily, knowing how ridiculous she must sound with her lips still wet with his kiss, his touch burning visibly on her face. "Unlike you, I don't go around kissing people I just met!"

"Neither do I," he muttered, shoving both fists deep into his pants pockets. He drew in a long, ragged breath, clearly struggling to recover from the effects of the last few moments. "And I didn't think that you did."

The bright headlights from a car revving up across the way fully illuminated the perplexed look on his face. "So why do you refuse to believe that I'm discriminating? Are you so unsure of yourself . . ."

"Let's not start *that* again," Danielle cut him off defensively, holding out a determined hand, which she barely kept from shaking. "I'll take my keys now."

"God," he sighed, shaking his head at her, "somebody must have done a real number on you to make you this defensive and insecure." He tugged the keys out of his pocket.

Danielle had assumed that when he'd shoved both fists in his pants pockets it was out of frustrated anger at her. She realized now that he'd been trying to hide the undeniable evidence of the effect of their kissing. She almost dropped the keys he'd just placed in her hand.

Wheeling around, she pulled her car door open and slid quickly inside. To her surprise, Devlin politely closed the door after her, but held on to the partially opened window. Bending his head down, he peered in at her.

"You really don't know how much woman you are," he said simply while Danielle shoved the key into the ignition and started up the car. "Obviously no man has ever shown you." He laughed softly, confidently. "I'm glad it's going to be me."

Danielle slammed her foot down on the accelerator. The car shot forward, forcing him back, and barely missed scraping the front fender of the Porsche as she pulled away.

She ground out an exasperated curse. Devlin Wilder was waving cheerfully at her in her rearview mirror.

3

~~~~~~~~~~~~~~~~~

Early the next morning, Danielle left Carmel for the studio-home Valmont had left her, along with the art gallery, in his will. The scenic drive south on Highway 1 to Big Sur was unlike anything she'd ever seen. Climbing abruptly from the canyon to emerge on high bluffs above the ocean, it hung as if suspended between the pounding, roaring Pacific on one side and the stone ramparts of the Santa Lucia mountains on the other. Clinging to the edge of the sheer cliffs from which it was cut, the narrow unpredictable road twisted and wound its way around the jagged fog-shrouded coastline, revealing rugged but staggeringly beautiful vistas at every turn.

Danielle couldn't have felt more removed from Boston if she'd landed on another planet. The seductive pull on her senses by the raw, monumental beauty surrounding her made keeping her eyes on the road difficult, in spite of the very real danger of going off a cliff.

She thought of Devlin Wilder. He was as different from Howard or Mark, her ex-husband, as this panorama of majestic mountains was from the skyline of a city. And every bit as overpowering. Like the raw, harsh beauty surrounding her, his kiss had touched something primitive in her. Something that she'd never known was there. She was grateful that seventy miles of rugged coastline separated them.

She wouldn't want to get involved with a man like Devlin Wilder at any time, but especially not now. She had come to Big Sur to be alone. She'd been feeling increasingly dissatisfied with her life for some time, and she didn't know why. Thanks to Valmont's surprising legacy, which included enough money to get settled and live comfortably for six months, she could get away and think about her life, try to discover what was missing from it.

If not, she could always go back to Boston. In her typically cautious manner, Danielle had suppressed the initial urge to burn her bridges behind her. The consulting firm she worked for as an efficiency expert had reluctantly allowed her a three-month leave of absence. With even greater reluctance, Howard had agreed to wait until September for her decision about their engagement. And her grandmother had merely sublet the apartment that Danielle rented from her to a vacationing college student. It would all be waiting there for her if she failed to find what she was looking for in Big Sur.

Danielle didn't find that as comforting as she thought she should.

According to Maggie Carson's excellent directions, which Danielle had been following religiously, Valmont's studio-home was over a mile away. But once she pulled off the main road onto an even more rugged one, they lay on the seat next to her, forgotten. Guided only by an unconscious compass somewhere inside her, she drove up the steep mountain. When she had negotiated a particularly sharp curve, it appeared before her—the stone and glass house where she'd spent the first six years of her life. She recognized the enormous slanted skylight from her recurring dreams.

Not bothering to remove her bags from the trunk of the Chevy she'd simply abandoned in the driveway, Danielle let herself into the house with a mixture of excitement and trepidation.

The interior of the house had the same stark look of the exterior due to the extensive use of natural rock and rough-hewn wood. If the condition of the living room was any indication, the house hadn't been lived in for years. Rusty water spots marred the beamed ceiling and stucco walls, and the acrid smell of mildew hung in the air. Sunlight streaked through dirt-encrusted windows, casting an eerie glow over the dustcovers which shrouded the furniture, adding to the abandoned, desolate look of the place.

As she wandered from room to room, long-forgotten childhood memories flooded Danielle, stirring up unexpected feelings of sadness and loss. She'd forgotten how happy she was during those few short years she'd lived there with her mother and Valmont.

Reverting to her typically analytical way of dealing with things that disturbed her, Danielle began coolly surveying the house and furnishings with an eye for their potential value should she decide to sell everything at the end of the summer and go back to her life in Boston. But she was caught unaware emotionally by the sight of the huge four-poster bed in the master bedroom. As a child, she couldn't wait to wake up in the mornings and rush into her parents' room to crawl under the covers with them for an hour of rough-and-tumble games.

Danielle tested the mattress with a critical hand. It needed a good airing but was more than serviceable. The Spanish colonial armoire and matching dresser and night tables were still in excellent condition. A couple of waxings and they'd be as good as new.

Continuing her inspection, she climbed the stone staircase which connected the living quarters to Valmont's studio. It had always been off limits when she was little, and like most forbidden things, had held a deep fascination for her. She couldn't help smiling to herself now as she recalled the hours she'd spent on those stairs, fantasizing about the mysteries and wonders she was sure were hidden behind that locked door.

Not even her wildest childhood fantasies could have prepared Danielle for the vision awaiting her on entering the vast, high-roofed studio. Standing in the light falling in a white-hot shaft from the great skylight was Devlin Wilder. He was wearing a pair of faded cutoffs and wielding a mallet and chisel, the powerful muscles of his naked arms and chest rippling with each blow. His bronze skin glistened with a fine sheen of perspiration and marble dust. With each rhythmic blow, the translucent chips twinkled like diamonds in the tawny hair matting his chest and lightly sprinkling his muscular arms and legs.

Danielle's audible gasp came as much from the sight of him as the shock of his being there. Devlin's surprise when he looked up at Danielle was even greater. The four-pound mallet with its stubby metal head glanced off the chisel, clipping his thumb.

"Damn!" His hand shot open in pain, dropping the steel chisel, which barely missed his sandal-clad foot.

"Oh, I'm sorry!" Danielle cried. "I didn't mean to distract you." Devlin muttered something unintelligible but clearly profane as she rushed over to him. "Are you all right?"

"OK . . . it's OK." He set the mallet down carefully on the stand next to the chunk of marble he'd been carving and assessed the damage to his thumb. "Now the other blood blister won't be so lonely," he joked, but Danielle could see the pain still darkening his eyes.

"I'm really sorry," she said sincerely. "Shouldn't you put something on that?"

"Nah, it's OK. Besides, it's worth it just to see you again." He smiled warmly, taking in the sight of her with obvious satisfaction, though she thought she detected a glimmer of wry amusement in his eyes when they skimmed over her navy blue tailored suit. "How did you manage to track me down?"

The look of concern on Danielle's face hardened into one of annoyance at his assuming that she'd come running after him. "I did not track you down," she protested. "You're not even supposed to be here. What are you doing in Valmont's studio?"

"Technically, it's *my* studio," he corrected her.

"What?"

"You really didn't know that?" He sounded oddly disappointed, as though he wished that she *had* come running after him. "I took it over from Valmont when he settled permanently in France . . . over six years ago."

It took Danielle a few moments before she was able to fully grasp the implications of his statement. She still hadn't recovered from the shock of his being there, and the sight of his half-naked body wasn't exactly helping her concentration. He was even more beautiful than she'd imagined.

Turning away from him, she made a quick survey of the studio which sprawled loftlike over the entire top floor of the house. She needed to assure herself that they were talking about the same place.

Unlike the house, the studio was obviously in full use. It was divided roughly in half: one side for stone carving, the other for clay modeling. The necessary tools and equipment lined the walls on either side, and a huge block of marble was suspended from pulleys attached to the ceiling. Several large modeling stands held works in progress, and charcoal sketches of a sensual-looking nude were attached to the cork wall.

"*This* is where you work?" She knew it was a dumb

question the moment she uttered it, but her mind simply refused to accept the fact that he was working in her father's studio.

"Six days a week," came the proud answer, "rain or shine."

Cursing Valmont under her breath (though she should have known that there would be complications with anything he'd been involved in), Danielle turned back to Devlin. "The studio belongs to me now," she informed him coldly.

"To you?" With bemused eyes he looked up from the skid mark the chisel had made on the marble he'd been shaping. "I don't understand."

"I inherited it from Valmont, along with the art gallery."

It was Devlin's turn to ponder implications while he studied Danielle intently. From his perplexed frown, she had the feeling that he'd just discovered something about her that didn't fit his original image of her.

"I didn't realize you knew Valmont," he said finally as he bent down to retrieve the chisel. The brilliant sunshine pouring through the skylight burnished his copper skin, highlighting the play of muscles in his powerful back. Danielle's mouth went dry. He straightened up again and faced her squarely. "Did you meet him in Paris?"

Instantly on the defensive, as she was whenever anyone tried to probe into her past, Danielle snapped, "Look, if you don't believe me, I've got the papers to prove it."

"I never said I didn't believe you. I just didn't know that you were so . . ." He paused, unconsciously checking the tip of the chisel with his thumb to make sure the fall hadn't blunted it, while he searched for the proper word. "So . . . close to Valmont that he would leave his studio to you."

Danielle couldn't keep a bitter little smile from twisting her lips at the thought that she and Valmont had been close, but she wasn't about to clarify matters. Whatever relationship Devlin Wilder assumed she had had with Valmont, it couldn't be more shameful than the one which had actually existed.

"The point is," she said evenly, determined to keep everything on a strictly impersonal basis, "the studio belongs to me now, so . . ."

"So you'll be living downstairs then," Devlin finished for her, excitement edging his tone.

"That's right," Danielle allowed patiently, "so you can understand why . . ."

"That's great!" His face lit up with a smile that was every bit as dazzling as the sunlight turning his tawny hair to gold. Danielle was blinded by him. She'd never known a man who felt things so intensely or showed his feelings so openly. "Then we're going to be neighbors," he continued.

"No, you . . . you don't understand," Danielle protested. "Now that I'm going to be living here, you won't be able to work here anymore."

"Why not? You won't get in my way."

"That's very big of you," Danielle muttered, "but what I meant was that *you're* going to be in my way."

"No, I'm not," he assured her pleasantly before pointing to the door through which she'd entered. "Except for that door, the studio is completely separate from the house. The entrance I always use . . ." He indicated the solid steel door at the far end of the studio. "Leads directly outside, in back of the house . . . where I also park my car." He shrugged his broad shoulders and they gleamed smooth and hard. "There won't be any problem."

The sight of him was problem enough, Danielle thought irritably, though she couldn't understand why that should be. She managed a cool "I'm afraid it's not that simple."

"Yes, it is," he disagreed softly. "You'll see." Danielle was sure she detected a double meaning in his words but the expression on his face contradicted her. "Do you need any help moving in?"

"No, thanks." She smiled sweetly. "Do you need any help moving out?"

He laughed. It bothered her that she enjoyed the rich, warm sound of his laughter. "Thanks anyway, but I'm not moving out." His tone was playful, but Danielle knew that he meant exactly what he said. If their first meeting had taught her anything about Devlin Wilder, it was how relentlessly persistent he could be in spite of his easygoing manner. But he wasn't going to get the better of her this time.

"Now look, Mr. Wilder," she began forcefully.

"After last night," he interrupted softly, "I think you can call me Dev." An ironic smile played on his mouth, but the message glowing in the golden depths of his eyes as they locked with hers was unashamedly sensual.

Maybe if she'd been prepared for the abrupt change in his manner, she wouldn't have been thrown so completely. As it was, Danielle had no defense against the memory of his kiss.

With an angry sigh, she turned and walked away from him. It was the only way that she could get herself back under control. She couldn't believe that he'd succeeded in making her feel so vulnerable again. In a way, she was glad he had—it strengthened her resolve to get him out of the studio.

"Mr. Wilder, I'm moving into the house today," Danielle resumed in her most businesslike tone of voice as she began walking around the studio with a determined air. "I'll be taking over the studio too, so you see . . ." She was brought up short by an exquisite clay study of a young girl trembling on the brink of womanhood. She was amazed that he was capable of such sensitivity.

Danielle dragged herself away from the statue and back to her original purpose. "So, I'm sorry but . . . you're going to have to find someplace else to work."

"You don't know what you're saying." An indulgent grin softened what could have been harsh words. She had the feeling that he was making an effort to be patient with her though she couldn't understand why. "Finding another studio, even here in Big Sur, isn't like renting a furnished room. It can take an artist years to build an ideal studio." He reached for the wet, soft stone that he kept on the stand next to the chunk of marble and began carefully sharpening the tip of the chisel. "It's taken me years to build *this* studio."

Danielle had only to look around to realize that he wasn't lying. She didn't know that sculpture required so many tools and materials, such intricate equipment. Moving all of it out of there, she suddenly realized, would be a mind-boggling, backbreaking job. For a moment, she actually felt guilty; she knew that she probably would have let anyone else stay on.

She struggled to find an appropriate excuse. How could she admit the truth to this man? She couldn't let him work there; it would mean seeing him every day, knowing every minute of the day that he was just upstairs. "I'm sorry" was finally all she could manage. "But that's how it is."

"That's how *what* is? I don't understand this." Slamming the chisel down on the stand impatiently, Devlin started toward her. "It isn't even to your own advantage. I'm sure you can use the rent money. It'll go a long way toward covering your expenses on the house and . . ."

"I'm sure it would," she cut him off coldly, "but privacy is more important to me than money right now."

"I wouldn't interfere with your privacy." He stopped directly in front of her, keeping her from walking away as she had intended. "All the years I've worked here, I've set foot in the house only three . . . maybe four times. And only at Valmont's invitation when he was staying over in Big Sur."

"It's not the same thing," she insisted.

"Of course it is," he countered earnestly. "I'd never presume to set foot in your home either. Unless you invited me." A roguish smile flickered across his face. "Don't misunderstand me, I'd love to get to know you . . . intimately. But I would never bother you."

But you do bother me, Danielle thought angrily. The way you look bothers me, the sound of your voice bothers me, everything about you bothers me and I don't know why . . . and *that* bothers me more than anything else!

She shook her head forcefully—maybe she could shake the absurd thoughts out and some sense back in. "No. I've made plans, and I can't . . . I won't let you wreck them."

"Were you planning on using the studio yourself?"

"Of course not," she said without thinking, and regretted it instantly.

"So you just want to get *me* out, is that it?" Oddly enough, he seemed more pleased than annoyed. "Do I really bother you that much?"

"Well, if that isn't your typical macho artist!" Danielle bit out contemptuously, pushing past him so he wouldn't see the giveaway blush flooding her cheeks. In her angry confusion, she almost walked smack into the human skeleton dangling from its supporting stand. "One of your ex-girl friends?" she couldn't resist tossing over her shoulder at him.

"No," he muttered curtly. He didn't seem to find her humor amusing this time. "I don't allow friends of any kind in my studio. This is where I work. When I feel like entertaining someone socially, I do it at home . . . not here."

"I see. So that bed . . ." She nodded in the direction of the studio bed that was up against the other wall. "*That's* just in case you want to take a little . . . nap?"

"*That's* a prop," he stated flatly. She could feel that he was rapidly running out of patience with her. "Just

like the chair or the . . . Is *that* what this is all about?"
He quickly covered the distance she'd deliberately put
between them. "Is that what's really bothering you?
You think I use the studio to . . . entertain other women
or make love to the models?"

"It doesn't bother *me*," Danielle assured him haughtily, but just the thought of it made her stomach knot up.

"But that's the kind of thing you assume goes on
here, isn't it?" he insisted, searching her face intently.

"It has nothing to do with that," she replied coldly
even though it had everything to do with that. Silently,
she reaffirmed her promise to herself that she would
never end up like her mother. "I told you, I have plans
for the studio."

"You never did say what they were." He obviously
didn't believe her. When she hesitated, he persisted
dryly, "What *are* you going to do with it?"

"Well, all this fantastic space . . ." Danielle struggled
to find a logical explanation to prove that her decision
had nothing to do with her feelings about him. She
settled for the first thing that popped into her head. "It
would make a great den."

"A den?" The flash of anger that twisted his rugged
features took her totally by surprise. "Valmont's studio
. . . a den? Are you crazy?" His hands balled up into
fists. "Don't you know that this is where Valmont did
the breakthrough work that gave him his place in the
history of American art?" He moved in on her. "And
you're going to turn it into a den? That would be like
turning a church into a whorehouse!"

The raw intensity of his emotions tautened every
muscle of his half-naked body as he towered over her.

Perspiration made his skin gleam like polished marble and he exuded a dizzying mixture of sweat and musky after-shave. But Danielle wasn't about to give him the satisfaction of making her back down—though she was shaking inside. "Well, some of us are worshipers at the exalted altar of the arts, and some of us aren't!" she snapped defensively.

"Why the hell did Valmont leave his studio to *you?*" he said contemptuously. "He obviously didn't know how you felt about . . ."

"Valmont knew *exactly* how I felt!" Danielle cut him off furiously. His comment had hurt her in a way she never would have believed possible. "I've never pretended to be anything but what I am!"

"And what is that?" He glared down at her. "You're obviously not just one of the philistines or even your average little gold digger. You're much too bitter for that!" He searched her face in that unnerving way that he had. "What are you?"

Without a word, Danielle spun around on her heels and walked away. She didn't stop walking until she got to the door and jerked it open. She was shaking from a barrage of emotions she couldn't even begin to define, and she had to concentrate to keep her voice steady and clear. "As far as you're concerned, Mr. Wilder, what I am is your landlord. As such, I'm giving you notice that you're to vacate these premises . . . today."

"And if I don't?" He didn't sound the least bit concerned, merely curious. It suddenly occurred to her that that had been his attitude all along. The sheer arrogance of the man!

"If you don't, I'll have you physically evicted!"

He smiled. "You can't have me evicted . . . physically or otherwise. Legally, you don't have one of those gorgeous legs to stand on." His mocking gaze moved slowly down her legs and even more slowly back up the length of her body to her burning face. "I have a lease with Valmont—which isn't up for another year and a half."

"A lease?" It never occurred to Danielle that he would have a lease. She didn't know that artists signed leases like normal people. "A lease," she repeated incredulously, "with Valmont?"

"If you don't believe me, I've got the papers to prove it," he drawled. "So if I were you, Ms. Adams, I wouldn't start picking out the wallpaper for that den just yet."

4

After having threatened to have Devlin Wilder physically evicted, Danielle couldn't help feeling foolish when she found herself sitting in his living room less than an hour later.

Not that she'd had a choice. Her telephone wasn't connected yet, and since he wouldn't allow one in his studio, she'd been forced to accept the offer of his home phone. But the calls which she'd placed to Valmont's American lawyer, as well as her own, had only proven Devlin correct. Short of blowing up the studio, there was no way she could get him out of there.

Danielle groaned inwardly. She could just imagine Devlin's smirk of satisfaction when she told him. She was seriously tempted to leave instead of just sitting there waiting for him to finish changing. Only the knowledge that she'd have to confront him sooner or later stopped her. Since she was forced to share her house with him, it was imperative that *she* set the perimeters of their relationship—business involvement, whatever—right from the start.

Danielle stood up. She wanted to be on her feet when he came in. With an impatient sigh, she began pacing the polished oak floor of the sunken living room. As upset as she was, she found herself looking around with interest.

Devlin's home, a sprawling rock, redwood and glass structure, had been designed to look like a natural extension of the cliff on which it perched some six hundred feet above sea level. Huge ceiling-to-floor windows, angled to admit maximum sunshine and great blue slices of sky, framed a breathtaking view of soaring headlands plunging into an ever pounding Pacific. The muffled roar of the ocean breaking itself to foamy bits against the jagged rocks below provided soothing background music.

Nature spilled indoors in a profusion of hanging and potted plants and the generous use of rock, wood and natural fibers. The raw silk love seats facing each other in front of the stone fireplace reminded Danielle of sand dunes because of their color and soft, sloping curves. They made her long to kick off her shoes and sink down into their almost voluptuous softness. A unique piece of swirling driftwood, which a glass top transformed into a cocktail table, stood on an authentic Navajo rug. The rest of the furnishings had been arranged in small, separate groupings, creating a casual but intimate ambience.

The color scheme was a subtle blending of earth

tones, from the lightest sand to the darkest brown. The only vivid color was provided by the painting hanging over the fireplace. From its harrowing intensity and the way the thick layers of bright red paint had been slashed on with a knife, she recognized it as an early Valmont. One of his best. It easily dominated the room as well as the rest of Devlin's impressive art collection. He also collected rare books, she realized before she was through, and had an extensive record library.

If Danielle had not met Dev and had to give her impression of the owner of the room, she'd have to say that he was uncompromisingly masculine, an individual who felt no need to prove himself to anyone. He was someone who preferred the simple, basic things in life, a man who was deeply sensitive to nature and beauty and wasn't ashamed to admit it.

That wasn't at all what she'd expected. It went against all her notions about artists in general, and Dev Wilder in particular. Reminding herself irritably that she wasn't there to get to know Devlin better, Danielle cut across to the glass doors that opened onto the patio.

At least out there all she had to contend with was the awesome power of nature, she thought wryly as she stepped outside. Her heels clicked loudly on the wooden floor boards as she walked past an open barbecue pit and cafe tables with colorful striped umbrellas to the far end of the patio.

A redwood deck, which ran the length of the house, extended beyond the edge of the cliff. Except for the stilts it perched on, it was completely suspended in space, Danielle realized when she looked over the railing at the sheer six hundred-foot drop to the raging, boulder-strewn surf. The sight was both frightening and exhilarating. Her heart beat faster and her fingers clung to the railing but her whole body strained forward in her eagerness to experience the raw, elemental power of nature.

"Don't enjoy the view too much," Dev warned half-jokingly from behind, startling her.

Danielle spun around to face him and a startled gasp caught in her throat. "Give me men to match my mountains," the California state motto, flashed in her mind when she saw Devlin silhouetted against the majestic mountains. Instead of diminishing him, they emphasized his larger-than-life quality. His craggy features could have been carved from the same rock and he seemed totally at one with nature. Yet, under that steady-as-a-rock exterior, Danielle sensed a wildness as primal as the harsh beauty surrounding them.

He'd changed into snug-fitting chinos, and his polo shirt hugged every muscle in his shoulders and chest. His hair was still damp from showering and he'd obviously gone to the trouble of shaving, although she hadn't noticed that he needed to before.

"I hope I didn't keep you waiting too long," he said as he came over to her. He was carrying a carafe of what appeared to be red wine with slices of lemon, lime and orange floating in it. A pair of balloon wine glasses dangled from his other hand. "I just made some sangria," he explained, setting the goblets down on the table nearest her. "I thought you might like some." He made a circular motion with the pitcher, sending ice cubes and citrus slices swirling around. "It's very refreshing." He smiled appealingly, the perfect host. He seemed to have forgotten that they were arguing less than an hour ago.

Danielle hadn't. "Nothing for me, thanks." Accepting the sangria would have put things on a friendly basis between them—exactly what he had in mind, she felt sure—while she was determined to keep everything on a strictly impersonal basis. "Mr. Wilder, the only reason I agreed to wait for you was so . . ."

"Oh, that's right," he interrupted as if she'd just reminded him of something which had completely slipped his mind. "Did you make your calls?"

"Uhh . . . yes," she mumbled reluctantly.

"What? I didn't hear you."

"Yes!"

He paused in the middle of filling his glass to slant her a droll look and ask pointedly, "And?"

"And . . ." Danielle swallowed hard and pushed both hands into her jacket's patch pockets, but she looked straight at him. "You were right. Legally, there's nothing I can do to get you out of the studio."

Dev smiled. But it wasn't the self-satisfied smirk that she'd expected. It was a smile of sheer, undisguised delight. Somehow, that was even worse.

"So you see," Danielle resumed, determined to retain what little control she had of the situation, "since I'm forced to share the same house with you, I think we should get certain . . . things straight right from the start."

"Absolutely," he agreed as he went back to filling his glass. "You sure you won't have some?"

"No, really, I'm . . ."

"I made it especially for you."

"Look, I'm trying to find some sort of compromise in this impossible situation!" she snapped, exasperated.

"Believe it or not, so am I," he muttered wryly. "This dumb sangria is my feeble attempt at an apology." He looked directly into her eyes. "I'm really sorry I got mad at you before, but I couldn't understand your reasons for wanting me to give up the studio. I thought you were just being perverse." His gold-flecked eyes searched her startled face intently. "Now I think I understand why you acted that way."

Danielle stiffened defensively.

"I was thinking about it while I changed," he went on thoughtfully, as though he were going over it again in his mind while he poured the other glass of sangria. "I asked myself how *I* would feel if I were moving into my new home only to find that a total stranger had taken over the top floor . . . and refused to leave."

He paused to garnish both glasses with a slice of orange. Danielle was vaguely surprised that his large fingers could move with such delicacy.

"I'm sure I would have been pretty damned mad and upset myself," he admitted softly, offering her a glass of sangria.

Danielle felt oddly moved and a bit guilty, and so relieved that he hadn't guessed the truth that she accepted his "apology." He rewarded her with a warm, intimate smile.

"I've come up with a compromise of my own," he said, pulling out a chair for her with his free hand. When she hesitated about sitting down, he added, "Don't you want to hear it?"

"What sort of . . . compromise?" she asked suspiciously. She hoped that the way she sat on the edge of the seat, refusing to rest comfortably against the cushions, conveyed the message that she wouldn't be staying long.

Instead of sitting in one of the other chairs, Dev propped himself up against the edge of the table next to her, his long, muscular legs stretched out in front of him. He stared thoughtfully into the burgundy depths of his glass for a moment. She wondered whether he was reconsidering his offer.

"Let's try it for two weeks," he said finally. "If you still feel the same way at the end of two weeks, then I'll look for another studio."

Danielle all but gasped. "Are you serious?"

"Absolutely."

"But I thought you said that finding another studio would be very difficult."

He took a long, lusty gulp of sangria befor shrugging fatalistically. "That's my problem. Well, what do you say?"

"But why would you do such a thing if you don't have to?" Danielle insisted. She was sure he had an ulterior motive. It didn't make sense otherwise. "Especially when you're in the right, legally."

Dev nodded in agreement. "Legally, yes. But not morally."

"Morally?" A short, sarcastic laugh escaped her. "I thought all you artists were above morality."

"No, not *all* of us," he countered dryly, "just the ones you're obviously accustomed to. And I would appreciate it if you would stop including me in that category."

"I'm sorry, but I just can't understand why . . ."

"What's there not to understand?" he cut her off, leaning in on her unexpectedly as if compelled by some need to make her understand him. She caught the warm, musky scent of his skin. "My lease *is* legally valid, but it was an agreement that I made with Valmont. The property belongs to you now. It's your home so it's only fair that any decision about renting out the studio should be yours also."

"I see," Danielle murmured, even though she didn't. This was the last thing she would have expected from someone like him. She fell back against the cushions. Maybe if he weren't hovering over her like that, she'd be able to think clearly again.

"On the other hand," he went on. "I've put a lot of years and hard work into that studio, as I told you earlier, and I think it's only fair that you give me the chance to see if we can work it out." He smiled disarmingly. "I'm sure that we can, but if you still feel we can't two weeks from now . . . then I'll move out. OK?"

He straightened up again and, tense with anticipation, waited for her answer. Danielle took several thoughtful sips of sangria while trying to decide. She had to admit that what Dev was offering her was more than fair, it was absurdly generous. No matter which way she looked at it, she had nothing to lose. Or did she?

"Well, is it a deal?" He held his large, suntanned

hand out to her. Her pale, delicate one reached up to take it. "Do we declare a truce for the next two weeks?"

Danielle's hand froze in midair. "What do you mean . . . a truce?"

"A truce means no more fighting. It simply means acting like neighbors—which is what we are." He grinned wryly at her. "You know, like saying good morning or hello when we meet? Nothing too heavy."

"As long as it's understood that this is a strictly business arrangement."

"Strictly business—absolutely," Dev agreed a little too quickly. And he seemed just a bit too pleased with himself. "As long as we're on *your* property."

Danielle pulled her hand back. "And what does *that* mean exactly?"

"To put it in strictly legal terms," he intoned mockingly, "it means that if the party of the first part, which is me, can entice the party of the second part, which is you, away from said property . . ." He paused, and a slow, sensuous smile curved his full lips. "The 'strictly business' clause no longer applies."

"But you won't be able to entice me away," Danielle assured him proudly.

"Then you have nothing to worry about," he said just before it occurred to her that she wasn't on her property now. "Is it a deal?" He held his hand out again. "Two weeks?"

Danielle finished off her sangria, barely aware of the sweet and tart taste of it while she ran his offer quickly through her mind again. It seemed a simple enough choice—between being cold and distant toward him for the next year and a half, or being reasonably pleasant to him for the next two weeks and never seeing him again afterward.

"All right," she agreed. "Two weeks." What could possibly happen in two weeks? She was on to Devlin's considerable charms so she should have no trouble resisting them. Besides, she could resist anything for two weeks, Danielle reassured herself as she returned his handshake, including the irresistible Mr. Wilder.

She'd forgotten how incredibly warm and vibrant the touch of his hand was. The scratchy texture of his skin felt oddly erotic. In that instant the realization that she would be living just downstairs from where he worked, that she would be seeing him every day frightened her in a way she couldn't understand.

"Well, that's it then," she said, pulling her hand away. It had grown warm and moist in his. Her other hand was ice-cold as she thrust her empty goblet into his still outstretched hand and jumped to her feet.

"Some more sangria?" he offered.

"No, that's it for me," she stated flatly, looking around the patio with a troubled expression.

Devlin eased himself away from the table. "Something wrong?"

"My pocketbook," she explained without looking at him. "I thought I brought it out here, but I must have left it in the living room." Without hesitation, Danielle made straight for the glass doors.

She spotted her pocketbook the instant she stepped into the living room. It was where she'd obviously left it, in a corner of the sofa. When she retrieved it, she was amazed to find that her hands were trembling slightly. What on earth was the matter with her? she wondered irritably; she had merely agreed to be pleasant to him for the next two weeks, not to become his lover! But it took a few minutes and several deep breaths before Danielle was ready to go back outside.

She found Dev hunkering down in front of the open barbecue pit. In her absence he had managed to construct a pyramid of charcoal briquets.

"Did you find it?" he inquired casually, lighting a foot-long wooden match.

"What are you doing?" She didn't bother to conceal her amazement.

He shrugged his powerful shoulders. "Lighting the charcoal."

"I can see that," she muttered, "but . . ."

"This is that new charcoal that's ready to use in fifteen minutes," he said as if that explained everything. The pyramid burst into flames, emitting the sharp, unmistakable smell of lighter fluid.

"I meant *why* are you doing that?" Danielle asked impatiently since she felt she'd made it pretty obvious that she was ready to leave and dependent on him to drive her home.

"Because I'm hungry," he stated matter-of-factly. "I haven't eaten since breakfast and I assumed you hadn't either."

"But, I was . . ." Danielle started to protest.

"*Have* you eaten since breakfast?" He slanted her a look over his shoulder.

"No," she had to admit, and breakfast had been just a croissant and black coffee.

"I didn't think so, and I'm sure you don't have any food at the house," he added in that infuriatingly reasonable way of his. "So I figured I'd throw a couple of hamburgers on the grill. A purely neighborly gesture," he was quick to assure her before she could protest again. He turned to her with a purely neighborly smile and mocking eyes. "How are you at fixing salads?" he asked.

5

That won't do you any good," Dev said, watching as Danielle put a slice of raw onion on her hamburger. "That only works if the other person isn't having any." Reaching across the table with his fork, he scooped up a large slice of onion and plopped it down on his burger. "If both people eat raw onions, it just cancels out the taste."

The tone of his voice sought to assure her that he was only joking, but his gaze lingered on her mouth as though he were mentally tasting her again. For an instant, Danielle reexperienced the sensation of his lips on hers, the sweetly seductive way his tongue had eased past them to slowly savor every inch of her mouth.

"Are you speaking as an expert on raw onions or kissing?" she managed sarcastically as she reached for the ketchup which she was sure matched the color of her face.

"Raw onions, of course," he countered. "I don't consider myself an expert in the other department since I'm only as good as the person I'm kissing."

Danielle was tempted to assure him that he was being overly modest but decided not to pursue that particular line of conversation. She gave the ketchup bottle a good solid whack, sending a big red blob splattering all over her hamburger.

She was sorry that she'd let him talk her into staying for dinner, though it had seemed a perfectly sensible suggestion at the time and she'd enjoyed fixing it with him. But now that they were sitting across the table from one another, making it impossible for her to ignore his disturbing presence, she wasn't so sure.

Everything seemed to be sabotaging her efforts to keep their relationship on a strictly impersonal level. The multihued, striped umbrella, the red and white checked tablecloth and the fresh carafe of sangria—all helped create the illusion that they were sitting at a sidewalk cafe on the Left Bank of Paris. The ocean, which reflected the deepening colors of the late after-noon sky, was as smooth as the Seine in August. It had tired of slamming itself against the rugged cliffs and was now lapping tenderly at them with a slow hypnotic rhythm. Fog was beginning to roll in in gauzy waves, smoothing the jagged outline of the coast, wrapping itself around the great headlands. The only sounds came from the ocean murmuring below and the birds calling to one another from the wind-bent cypresses which clung to the sides of the sea wall.

In the middle of it all sat Devlin Wilder, looking wonderfully at ease, as if their being there together was the most natural thing in the world—inevitable even.

"So how will you go about finding another studio?" Danielle asked, deliberately steering the conversation away from the personal slant it had taken while she finished scraping the excess ketchup onto her plate.

"I'll deal with that problem when, and if, I have to," Dev replied smoothly before taking another lusty bite out of his hamburger.

Danielle had the feeling that he did everything that way—with that same hungry intensity. "What I don't understand is why you don't have a studio in your own home, like most artists."

"Discipline," he explained, spearing several lettuce leaves with his fork and devouring them in one gulp. "Umm, that's a really good dressing," he complimented her sincerely.

It annoyed her that she was pleased. "What do you mean . . . discipline?"

"I've always felt that having your studio where you live makes for lazy work habits. I prefer getting up in the mornings, getting dressed and leaving the house . . . as I did when I was still going to the office." He shrugged self-consciously. "I guess it's a habit I acquired while I was in my family's import-export business."

Danielle almost choked on her hamburger. "You were in business?"

"I'll have you know I was a very respectable businessman for almost ten years. A veritable pillar of the community." He chuckled self-mockingly, as though it were as difficult for him to believe at this point.

Danielle was fully aware that he'd managed to turn the conversation into a personal one again, but her curiosity about him kept her from stopping him—or herself. "What happened to make you . . . change?"

"I'd always wanted to be an artist," he explained while assembling another one of his—what could only be described as a Dagwood burger. "But my family was in business, and as the only son I couldn't let my father down, so I agreed to carry on the family tradition." Devlin shook his head at the memory of himself as he was then and looked over at Danielle with droll amber eyes. "I was so square back then that even you would have loved me. I did everything that was expected of me, including marrying the right girl."

It had never occurred to Danielle that he might be married. He certainly didn't act as if he were—but what artist did? She should have known that someone as devastatingly attractive as he was would have been grabbed up years ago. It was better that way, she decided, using her napkin to dab at the drops of wine she'd just spilled on the checked tablecloth. Safer.

"Then, the year I turned thirty," he continued, still squinting down at his culinary creation in order to decide what was missing, though he'd put everything on it except the proverbial kitchen sink, "my father died. A heart attack. He was only fifty-four years old." There was no emotion in his voice but his hand hesitated as he was about to place more pickles on his hamburger. "I had no children of my own, so I guess I just didn't feel obligated to keep up the family tradition anymore." A sad smile pulled down the corners of his mouth. "Or maybe I finally realized that time was too precious to waste . . . so I decided to pursue the life I'd always dreamed of."

"But how did your wife and family feel about that?" Danielle asked in spite of herself, hoping that she'd managed to sound only mildly interested.

"Everybody thought I was crazy to walk away from what they all thought was an enviable life. I had everything: money, social position, the perfect wife. But you see . . ." He leaned toward her, across the table, his Dagwood burger forgotten. "I'd been living *their* version of my life, and it had been eating away at me for years. But I couldn't make any of them understand that."

"I know exactly what you mean." Danielle leaned toward him unconsciously. *"That's* exactly how everyone reacted to my plans to come out and live here in Big Sur. My grandmother—she's the one who raised me—thinks I should get my head examined to even consider giving up all my 'advantages' in Boston."

Dev laughed. "My wife went so far as to make an appointment with a psychiatrist for me."

"Are you still married?" Danielle blurted out before she could stop herself.

"No." He sat back up and grabbed the triple-decker burger in both hands. "Blythe could never have given up her career and the society life she loves to move out here with me," he said between bites. "She runs the import-export business now—better than I ever did. She's one hell of a businesswoman," he admitted freely, surprising Danielle with his lack of resentment.

"The divorce was an amicable one," he explained, obviously aware of her reaction. "Just as our marriage had been. I think that's when I realized that we'd never really loved one another, at least not in a passionate, deeply committed sense." Reaching for his wine glass, he finished off what was left of his sangria in one gulp. "Up to that point, I'd actually believed, along with all our friends, that we had a good marriage. Don't misunderstand me, Blythe is a lovely, intelligent woman of great charm . . . and we genuinely cared about one another, but something . . . vital was missing."

He paused to stare intently into his empty goblet. Danielle had the feeling that he'd never spoken about this to anyone before and that made her feel uncomfortable yet strangely elated at the same time.

"There was a . . . a void at the core of our relationship . . . always had been," he went on, unable to stop himself now that he was finally putting it into words. "At least, that's how *I* felt about it. Everybody else said that what I was looking for in a relationship doesn't exist in real life. But I refused to believe that." He went silent for a moment before looking back up at her with a self-conscious and immensely appealing grin. "My family still thinks I'm crazy."

"My family has never forgiven me for getting a divorce either," Danielle found herself admitting for the first time. "The fact that Mark, my ex-husband, was consistently unfaithful was not considered an adequate reason."

"You're kidding? I'd hate to hear what they consider an adequate reason!" He laughed, and she couldn't help joining in. She was surprised that *he* would feel that way and even more surprised that she could laugh at something which had caused her such pain that she'd never been able to talk about it.

"I was actually accused of betraying the family honor by having the first divorce on record. Do you believe that—in this day and age?" Danielle laughed again. Why hadn't she realized before how absurd the whole thing had been instead of feeling so guilty about it? "Those were Grandmother's exact words. I had betrayed the family honor just like my mother and . . ." Danielle stopped herself just in time. She couldn't believe that she was exposing her most intimate secrets to a stranger. "And all because I have 'unrealistic expectations' about love and marriage," she finished lamely.

"You too? Well, it looks as if we've got something in common, after all," he said with great satisfaction, as though he'd just scored a major point in his favor.

It threw Danielle completely. She refused to believe that she could have anything in common with Devlin Wilder, or with any artist. She started pushing her salad around on her plate with her fork. "I don't think we're talking about the same thing."

"Of course we are," he said flatly, annoyance edging his tone. He was obviously a man who didn't like playing games—or women who did. "You know we are."

Danielle decided to ignore that in favor of finishing her salad. But even though she wasn't looking at him, she could feel him studying her intently in the sudden, nerve-racking silence. It was all she could do to finish the salad instead of throwing it at him, plate and all.

"So what's wrong with Howard," Dev asked matter-of-factly as he refilled both wine glasses.

"Nothing's wrong with Howard," Danielle was quick to assure him once she got over her initial surprise that he'd remembered her fiancé's name. "He's a very successful lawyer, good-looking, charming and . . ."

The ironic smile playing on Dev's mouth made Danielle realize that she was repeating his description of his ex-wife almost word for word, exposing the same lack of deep feeling which, she'd only recently admitted to herself, was what was missing in her relationship with Howard. That was also the reason she'd been unable to become intimate with him, despite all his pressuring these last few months, and why she'd finally postponed the wedding.

"There's nothing wrong with Howard," she repeated stubbornly, ignoring the feeling that Devlin Wilder could read every thought in her head. He was certainly trying hard enough.

"Then what are you doing here?" he asked pointedly.

Danielle wasn't sure whether he meant here in Big Sur or here having dinner with him. Either way, it was none of his business. "I just don't want to rush into marriage . . . as I did the first time," she explained, furious at herself for even bothering since she certainly didn't owe him any explanation.

The mocking look in his eyes made it clear that he didn't believe a word of it anyway. Slowly twirling the stem of his glass, he continued to study her intently. "And what about Mark?" he asked casually. "Was he an artist?"

"I admit to being somewhat impulsive, but I'm not self-destructive," she muttered sardonically. "What on earth made you think that?"

"Well, you have such a lousy opinion of artists," he noted ruefully. "You must have been burned pretty badly. Who's to blame for that . . . Valmont?"

Danielle tensed visibly but made a quick recovery. "I've really enjoyed playing twenty questions," she managed as she pushed away from the table and got to her feet. "But, if you don't mind, I'd like to go home now."

"I don't mind," he agreed pleasantly. "But I'd like to finish my dinner first." Reaching for the wooden utensils, Dev helped himself to another hefty portion of salad.

Danielle drew in a long, hard breath and mentally counted to ten. "Let me know when you're ready," she got out tartly, then turned quickly on her heels and walked over to the far end of the patio. Leaning over the railing with her back to Dev, she let out a string of curses under her breath that she never would have believed herself capable of. Never in her life had she known such an irritating, aggravating, impossible man!

Dev let go with a few choice curses of his own, sending his chair screeching against the wooden deck as he came striding over to her. "Why do you always change the subject when Valmont's name comes up?"

Danielle turned on him angrily. "Why do you keep prying into my personal life?"

"I'm not prying," he protested. "I'm just trying to find out what I'm up against. You refuse to give me a chance because of this resentment you have against artists . . . and I'm trying to find out why you feel that way."

"I'm just not dazzled by the artistic temperament, that's all." She gave what she hoped looked like a careless shrug. "Why should that bother you so much? From what I saw last night, there are plenty of other women who are."

"What are you talking about?" He seemed genuinely confused.

"Oh, come on now," she bit out contemptuously. "Look, you've gotten what you wanted—everything you ever dreamed of. You're a successful artist, admired and surrounded by beautiful women who are only too eager to throw themselves at you . . ."

"That kind of life," he cut her off dryly, "isn't as enviable as it appears. The men collect art and their bored wives collect artists. It's all an ego trip."

Danielle was caught off-balance by the surprising bitterness in his voice. The defensive comeback she was readying disintegrated before she could put the words together.

"And you're wrong about my having everything I ever dreamed of," he muttered ruefully. "My work . . . yes. That's the best thing in my life right now. But I still haven't found the . . . emotional satisfaction I was looking for." He moved closer to her, intense amber eyes searching her face as though he hoped to find what he was looking for there.

Without wanting to, Danielle felt herself being drawn to the longing in him. He moved closer still, so close that she could feel the heat emanating from his body. The sensual intensity he projected was almost palpable.

"That's what I was trying to tell you before," he breathed.

Danielle stepped back. She'd never felt so totally vulnerable in her life. She couldn't believe that he was doing this to her again. Turning away from him, she struck back in self-defense. "Oh, I'm sure you get plenty of . . . satisfaction!"

"Stop that!" Dev exploded. "And look at me!" His fingers dug painfully into the soft flesh of Danielle's upper arm as he turned her around to him forcefully. "I want you to see *me*, to hear what *I'm* saying!" His other hand shot out to grab her free arm, making it impossible for her to move although she was already stunned by the emotional intensity of his outburst. "I want you to respond to *me*—not to some goddamn ghost from your past!"

He pulled her hard up against him and his mouth came down bruisingly on hers. His arms locked around her until she could barely breathe, crushing her against the long, taut length of him as if he meant to force her to feel every part of him, to wipe out the memory of any other man and imprint himself on her instead.

Danielle might have been able to withstand a purely physical assault on her senses but was helpless against such an emotional one. Her mouth opened under the fierce demand of his, allowing the possessive thrust of his tongue. The anger suddenly went out of his kiss only to be replaced by an even more frightening hunger.

He released her as abruptly as he'd grabbed her, causing her to stagger back several steps. "OK, you can get made at me now," he rasped breathlessly. "At least it's because of something that *I* did to you.

"Go ahead," he insisted when she didn't, couldn't, react. "Yell, scream . . . hit me if you want." He even took a step toward her to make it easier for her.

Overwhelmed by a barrage of conflicting emotions and sensations which she'd never experienced, couldn't begin to deal with, Danielle could only stand there and try not to shake.

Dev noticed that she was biting down on her bottom lip to keep it from trembling, and he caught a glimpse of the fear in her wide violet eyes just before she looked away. "Oh, Christ!" He reached out a hand that was shaking as much as hers only to let it drop to his side with a kind of self-disgust. "I'm . . . sorry."

Danielle pushed past him as she finally got the use of her legs back. "I think it's pretty obvious," she bit out shakily, "that there's no way this is ever going to work out so . . ."

"Oh, no, you don't!" Dev came stalking after her, easily overtook her and placed himself between her and the glass doors. "We made a deal."

"Which you just broke!" she cried angrily.

"I did not," he protested, all innocence, making Danielle seriously consider throwing the carafe of sangria at him. It was within arm's reach.

She took a long, steadying breath instead. "You agreed that this was going to be a strictly business arrangement."

"Only on your territory," he reminded her with a feral smile. "You're on my turf now." He stepped away from the glass doors, moving in on her with intent, and Danielle was sure that he meant to kiss her again. She felt a moment of pure panic because she didn't know if she'd able to resist him if he did.

Something must have decided him against it because he stopped himself—though his gaze lingered regretfully on her mouth. "Come on." He sighed heavily. "I'd better take you home now because if I don't . . ." He didn't finish the sentence. He didn't have to. They both knew exactly what he meant.

"I'd rather take a cab." Danielle's hand was trembling again as she picked up her pocketbook. "Will you call one for me, please?"

"That's not necessary," he insisted softly. "We made a deal and I intend to keep it. I'm going to play it your way for the next two weeks."

"After what just happened," Danielle countered defensively, "give me one good reason why I should believe you."

"Because if there's one thing I've learned as an artist, it's that you can't force a work of art. It's something that has a life of its own, that has to grow at its own pace . . . just like love." He smiled at her then, a disarming smile full of hope and longing with just a hint of grim determination.

Would she really be able to resist this man for two weeks? Danielle wondered fearfully before she allowed him to escort her to his car.

6

~∞∞∞∞∞∞∞∞∞~

Danielle dragged herself out of bed the next morning after a troubled, dream-filled sleep. She tried telling herself that her restlessness was only natural since it was her first night back in her childhood home, but the face that had haunted her dreams was one from the present, not the past. Mercifully, her pre-coffee brain was incapable of functioning except on the most rudimentary level, so she didn't have to deal with her feelings about her dreams or about seeing Dev Wilder later on. It was all she could do to get the rusted-out shower working.

It took her a good half-hour before she succeeded, and even then the erratic stream of water was yellowish and came in only two temperatures: ice-cold or scalding-hot. The first day of her life in Big Sur was starting off just great!

Danielle was seriously wondering whether her shower was an omen of things to come until, rummaging frantically through the kitchen cabinets, she found a sealed container of ground coffee. She could have wept with relief. Normally, she could have twitched her way through the rest of the morning without a cup of coffee—but not today. Today promised to be anything but normal and she would need all the help she could get.

She was surprised to find the cupboards stocked with an assortment of canned goods, just as she had been the night before to find the linen closet filled with clean sheets and towels, all neatly folded and wrapped in protective plastic. Neither the gas nor the electricity had been disconnected. Obviously, Valmont wanted his houses, like his mistresses, to be available to him at all times.

She certainly couldn't fault him when it came to interior decorating, she thought as she made the coffee. In keeping with the rest of the house, the kitchen had an authentic Spanish colonial flavor. Intricately carved pine cabinets lined the wall over the sink and concealed modern appliances. The hand-painted ceramic tiles that lined the countertop and continued up the wall to the cabinets matched the vibrant color of the clay tile floor. The large table in front of the raised-hearth fireplace and the high-backed chairs circling it were also of pine, and clearly antiques.

The most unique feature of the room was the large arch-crowned window. Like all the windows in the house, it was set into a deep opening in the twenty-six-inch-thick adobe wall. The sill of patterned brick formed a window seat wide enough for Danielle to sit on and stretch her long legs out comfortably before her. The grocery list she'd started lay forgotten in her lap as she savored the fresh-brewed coffee and the stunning view of rolling, pine-studded mountains. The early morning fog had burned off and a brilliant, cloudless sky stretched out to infinity.

She was on her second cup of coffee when, at precisely eight-thirty, she saw Dev's white Jaguar XJ-S negotiating the final curve in the driveway. Her throat tightened automatically, making it difficult to swallow. Her first impulse was to jump up and run into another room, but he'd already spotted her.

Danielle decided to concentrate on the shopping list while he parked the sleek sports coupe directly in front of the window. But no matter how hard she tried to concentrate, she was still intensely aware of him as he got out of the car and ambled over to the window. She continued staring at the list, for all the world too engrossed to be aware of anything going on around her. Dev rapped on the windowpane, rattling Danielle as much as the glass.

With a silent curse, and a surprise reaction straight out of a B movie, Danielle looked up at him. Even through the dust-streaked window he gleamed all golden in the brilliant sunlight. He waved at her cheerfully, mouthed a neighborly good morning and then bounded up the outside stairs, disappearing into his studio as promised—but not before she caught a flash of golden mockery in his eyes. She cursed loud and clear that time.

Resolutely forcing all thoughts of Devlin Wilder out of

her mind, Danielle spent the rest of the morning assessing the amount of work and money needed to make the house livable again. Her experience as an efficiency expert proved invaluable as she quickly roughed out a budget and a daily work schedule. There were no major repairs as far as she could see, so she could fix up the house herself and expenditures would be kept at a minimum. She didn't plan any drastic decorating changes either, since she was forced to admit that she couldn't have improved upon Valmont's efforts. But she did plan to add a few personal touches, especially in the bedroom, which she felt could use a softer, more feminine touch. She already visualized the perfect wallpaper and knew exactly the kind of drapes that . . .

A strange sound intruded on her thoughts as she continued jotting down her ideas excitedly. A more determined rap, this time on the bedroom window nearest her, finally broke her concentration. She turned toward the source of irritation to find Dev grinning at her through the dusty panes. He was holding up one end of a large, rectangular chest in one hand; the other end rested precariously on the windowsill. With his free hand, he was motioning to her to open the window so that he could say something.

Wondering what he was up to now, Danielle crossed warily over to him. The window was stuck so it took a couple of minutes before she could slide the top half down. "Yes?" she asked, suspiciously.

"I was just about to have lunch," he explained, grabbing the other end of the chest just as it slid off the windowsill. Danielle realized that it was a cooler, the kind that people take on picnics or to the beach. "I always have my lunch outdoors, weather permitting," he went on. "I wondered if you'd . . . care to join me?" He smiled again, the tentative smile she found so at odds with that strong, craggy face, and so very appealing.

"Lunch?" Danielle murmured. She hadn't realized it was that late. She'd meant to go shopping for fresh food before she got caught up in her redecorating plans.

"Nothing fancy," he said loudly, "just some cheeses and cold cuts."

She wondered why he was practically shouting, then realized that he was trying to project his voice through the mere three-inch opening she'd allowed in the window. He reminded her of a kid with his nose pressed up against the glass of a candy store. She smiled in spite of herself. She was about to ask him why he hadn't simply come to the front door but remembered his promise never to set foot in the house unless she invited him. She found that touching in a funny kind of way.

"All right," she agreed. "But just this once," she added quickly as defense against the devastating smile he rewarded her with. "And only because I had pork and beans for breakfast and I'm not looking forward to eating lunch out of a can too."

"Nothing fancy, just some cheeses and cold cuts" proved to be something of an understatement. They enjoyed a lunch of sinfully rich Brie and Camembert, a country pâté and smoked ham with crusty French bread, and a chilled bottle of imported Chardonnay. The spot Devlin selected for their picnic was a cypress-shaded knoll that edged a cliff overlooking the surf-carved coastline.

"This certainly beats the automat," Danielle couldn't help observing. And this man certainly beat every man she'd ever known—she kept that disturbing observation to herself.

Since Dev went out of his way to keep the conversation casual, Danielle was able to relax in his presence for the first time since they'd met, especially if she didn't look at him but concentrated on her food or the view. There were a few times when she was actually in danger of enjoying herself.

Afterward, Dev returned to his studio and Danielle went back to sorting out what could be salvaged from the remnants of her childhood. At precisely four-thirty Dev materialized outside her bedroom window again to ask whether she needed anything before he left for the day. When she assured him that she didn't, agreed that she would call him at home if she did, and turned down his dinner invitation, he wished her a pleasant good evening and left.

That first day set the pattern for the rest of the week, with Danielle taking turns making lunch. She told herself that it wasn't the same thing as dating, that it was merely a pleasant break in their workday. Besides, he was the only person she really knew in Big Sur and he'd been so helpful, answering all her questions, directing her to the best stores for food or the supplies she needed to fix up the house.

He seemed to have accepted the fact that she wouldn't go out with him, though he still asked her to dinner every evening before he left, but he hadn't made a move toward her since the barbecue at his place. A physical move, that is, because the very sight of him, the lusty way that he ate and the wide open warmth of his smile all seduced her. If he had been physically aggressive with her, she would have been able to defend herself against him, but she had no defense against his natural charm, his quirky sense of humor and the surprising depth and warmth of his personality. And she found herself looking forward to those lunches, which were getting longer and longer, even though all they did was talk.

Danielle didn't realize how much she looked forward to them until Sunday as she ate a solitary lunch on the window seat in the kitchen. She would never have believed that a day could be so agonizingly long, that silence could be so oppressive. The worst part of it was that she couldn't stop wondering what Dev was doing . . . and who he was doing it with. She scrubbed the kitchen tiles until she saw her exhausted reflection in them but she still had trouble sleeping that night.

By the middle of the second week, instead of going right back to his studio after lunch, Dev started helping Danielle with some of the heavier chores. He explained that he was in the thinking stage which always preceded his work on a new sculpture. Danielle's excuse to herself was just as logical: now that she'd started painting, she wasn't up to moving all that heavy furniture by herself. What she couldn't understand was why, after a long day of the most strenuous physical activity, she was having trouble sleeping at night.

"Need any help?" Dev's amused inquiry interrupted Danielle as she was trying, unsuccessfully, to hitch her leg over the top of the kitchen sink. "What are you doing?"

With an exasperated sigh, she glanced over her shoulder at him. She hadn't realized that she'd left the top part of the Dutch door open. Dev was visible only down to his lean hips but still managed to look larger-than-life, since his broad shoulders and chest took up most of the width of the upper doorway. "What does it look like I'm doing?"

"It looks like you're trying to take a bath in the kitchen sink."

"Exactly." Danielle laughed. "Doesn't everybody?" As frustrated as she was, she was fully aware of how ridiculous she must look hopping about on one leg while trying to sling the other one over the waist-high counter.

"A bath, huh? Would you like me to wash your back?" She was sure that he'd meant it jokingly but it came out with a darker undertone. Following the direction of his suddenly intense stare, she discovered that her terry cloth robe had opened in front, exposing the length of her bare leg clear up to her equally bare hip.

Danielle dropped her leg to the floor and quickly adjusted her robe. "Is it four-thirty already?" She concentrated on working her toes back into her rubber thongs.

"Yeah," he murmured. "Time flies even when you're not enjoying yourself." The way Dev's eyes moved over her body, she was sure he knew that she was naked under the robe. Tearing his glance away, he stared up at the ceiling. "You did a great job on that ceiling." He was clearly making an effort to keep the tone of his voice casual. "And I see you managed to paint yourself as well."

"I know." Danielle laughed again but there was a nervous edge to it this time. Her hand flew self-consciously to her thick black hair, which was piled on top of her head and speckled with tiny white dots of paint, as was her face. "I tried to take a shower," she added, tugging the top of her robe closed, "but the shower head broke. It's all rusted out and when I tried to adjust it . . . it just broke right off."

Dev chuckled understandingly, her peculiar behavior having suddenly become clear to him. He leaned casually against the closed bottom half of the door. "You're welcome to use the shower at my place."

Danielle clutched the top of her robe even tighter. "Oh, no . . . it's OK."

"You've nothing to be afraid of." Dev straightened up again and she thought she saw a flicker of annoyance cross his face. "You should know that by now."

"No, it's not . . . that," she scoffed lightly but the strain in her voice was obvious even to her. What she couldn't tell Dev was that she was just as afraid to trust herself with him in such an intimate situation. "I'll make do . . . with my little sink."

"I don't see how a big girl like you is going to make

do with a little sink like that." His attempt at a joke was as dismal as hers. Suddenly, the very air between them seemed charged with electricity. Danielle could feel the sparks skittering along her nerve ends.

"I was planning on doing it in sections," she rattled on, "first one leg, then the other, then a . . ." His darkening gaze moved over her as though he were visualizing every part of her body and the words stuck in her throat.

Dev turned away abruptly to stare at a grove of redwoods in the distance. "There is an alternative . . . one I use myself often," he said evenly when he looked back at her. "Do you have a bathing suit?"

"A bathing suit? Sure, but . . ."

"Great. Go put it on," he ordered as he took off for his Jaguar, which he always parked in front of the kitchen window.

"Hey, wait a minute," Danielle called after him. Rushing over to the door, she leaned out the open half as Dev was snapping the glove compartment shut.

"I always keep a swimsuit in here." To prove it, he waved a triangle of blue lycra at her. Starting for the stairs, he added dryly, "I'd better change in the studio today."

"Look, I . . ."

Dev paused midway up the stairs. "You do want to get that paint off you?"

"Of course," she admitted—the paint and the grime and the sweat, but that wasn't the problem. "I'd just like to know where we're going. Is there a pool around here?"

"It's more like a . . . natural shower." When Danielle still hesitated, Devlin added pointedly, "It's on *your* property."

"Is it much farther?" Danielle asked, following closely behind Devlin. The winding mountain road they'd taken from the house had narrowed to a foot trail which, judging from the undergrowth trying to reclaim it, was rarely used.

"Why do you ask?" He slanted her an amused look over his shoulder. "Afraid I'm leading you astray?"

She laughed breathlessly. "Terrified."

"Don't tell me you actually trust me." He laughed in return, a deep, rich laugh. The steep climb and thin mountain air obviously had no effect on him.

"Not necessarily," she countered jokingly, "but there isn't very much you can do here." With a carefree wave of her hand, she indicated the thick foliage surrounding them. There was barely enough room between trees to stand, let alone indulge any sexual inclinations.

"Don't count on it." His eyes flashed a warning that shivered up her spine. "I'd find a way."

Danielle didn't doubt him for a second. With a shock, she realized how close to the surface his real feelings about her were, how fragile was the civilized veneer beneath which he concealed them. She resolutely shut out the stream of sensual images his comment had evoked in her mind. She was unable to control the physical reaction—a wild fluttering of wings—in the pit of her stomach.

She chose to disregard his comment, as if that would make the sexual tension between them disappear. "I really can't imagine that there would be a body of water in this forest."

"Trust me."

What choice did she have? Danielle thought nervously. Still, Dev had kept his promise these last two weeks and he'd had plenty of opportunities to make his move. He certainly didn't need to take her out into the woods to try anything. Then why was she trembling?

Damn him! Damn him that he could do this to her with just a look, one comment!

They continued on in silence, except when Dev pointed out a bird or some furry creature that Danielle hadn't noticed. She was too busy watching *him*. She kept forcing herself to look up at the trees swaying in the strong, fragrant breeze, to notice how the smaller plants strained upward to catch a slice of sunshine streaming through the branches overhead. But always her eyes went back to Dev as he continued leading the way.

It was as though Danielle's stubbornly logical mind were determined to find the reason why this particular man should have such an effect on her. She'd met handsome men before, even briefly dated a few, a couple of them better-looking than Dev in an even-featured way. But she'd never met anyone so intensely, compellingly attractive. And never in her life had she been so aware of a man on a purely physical level. What was it about *this* man? she wondered resentfully as her eyes went over him inch by inch.

Was it the sensuous play of muscles in his powerful shoulders and back? Or the corded strength of his thighs, which strained against his jeans with every movement, making her long for the feel of them wrapped around her? Or could it be the forceful yet surprisingly graceful way that he moved, the vibrant sexuality he projected so effortlessly?

No, it was more than that.

But what was it exactly? Was it the strong, dramatic lines of his face, his remarkable expressiveness? The unique golden color of his eyes? Or was it his soft, sensitive mouth and the way he had of smiling that warmed her through and through? Was that it? Danielle felt sure that if she could just figure out exactly what it was, it would lose its effect on her and . . .

The trail came to an abrupt end at an embankment, ending Danielle's troubled musings as well.

"There it is." Dev was pointing to a waterfall at the foot of the embankment. "There's your natural shower."

"Oh, my God," Danielle gasped at the sight of it. "I didn't know such places still existed in this world."

"It's really something, isn't it?" He smiled warmly at her, obviously pleased that she shared his feeling about what was clearly a very special place to him. "I come here often," he went on as he began unbuttoning his blue work shirt. "Whenever I want to get away from it all." His broad fingers hesitated on the last button. "But it's the first time I've ever brought anyone else here."

"I can understand why you'd want to keep it to yourself," Danielle replied, deliberately choosing to misunderstand him, to deny the rush of warmth that went through her at his words. "It's incredibly beautiful." She caught the hurt look on Dev's face just before she rushed headlong down the embankment toward the waterfall.

The lacy cascade, which plunged from a source high in the mountains, tumbled over a series of rocky ledges into a sparkling creek. It nestled in a thick grove of redwoods that all but blocked out the sky. Sunlight streaked through the branches of the giant trees like the ethereal shafts of light piercing the stained glass windows of a Gothic cathedral. Ferns and wild flowers carpeted the forest floor and perfumed the air.

Totally awed by the primeval beauty that surrounded them, Danielle felt as though they'd stumbled back in time to the dawn of Earth. A sudden gust of wind skipped over the water, sending out a refreshing spray, an irresistible invitation. Slipping eagerly out of her black-and-white print wraparound, Danielle turned to tell Dev that she was going in the water but the words caught in her throat.

Stripped down to his bathing suit, Dev stood at the top of the embankment, squinting up into the late afternoon sun. The sight of him silhouetted against the sky stirred Danielle deeply. He exuded the same raw beauty and power as their primal surroundings and it excited and frightened her at the same time. But she couldn't tear her gaze away. Her eyes moved over every line and curve of his body, over his sun-dappled skin with a kind of fearful wonder. She might have been Eve seeing Adam for the very first time.

Dev's body tensed instinctively as if he sensed the intensity of the emotions overwhelming her before he saw it on her face. His own gaze moved searchingly over Danielle's body, burning through the thin fabric of her black maillot. When his eyes locked with hers, she read the blatant message in their golden depths. The whole world went silent. For an endless moment all she could hear was the blood pounding in her ears. Then the sound of rushing water came back in, and the helpless rustling of the leaves as another powerful gust of wind shook them. A fresh spray of water, icy dots melting on contact with her burning skin, jolted Danielle out of her trance. She spun around and, skipping over the moss-covered rocks leading to the bottom ledge, plunged into the waterfall.

It was as clear and cold as spring water, shocking her whole body alive, making her skin tingle all over. She laughed and shrieked like a child under its delicious assault. She couldn't remember ever feeling so free. Shaking her head, she sent her long, thick hair whipping around her face and neck. When it was soaking wet, she slicked it back with both hands and and offered her face up to the surprisingly soft, frothy water, stretching her arms up as though she meant to embrace the lacy cascade spilling over her.

Danielle's gesture was an unconscious imitation of Dev's statue. She was unaware of the sensuality she projected until she saw it reflected in Dev's eyes when he joined her in the water.

Without a word, as if language hadn't been invented yet in this primeval world, Dev grabbed her, pulling her hard up against him. Danielle gasped as she felt his heated skin on her chilled flesh, the sudden burning crush of his mouth. Possessive arms wrapped around her, striving to gather her all up, to surround her totally.

The roaring sound of the waterfall seemed to echo the rush of blood pounding through her veins as his mouth moved on hers with a hunger that was almost frightening in its intensity. Finally released, the sensual longing for her that he'd been suppressing these last two weeks was as uncontrollable as the torrent of water pouring over them. It shook Dev's powerful body and went through Danielle like a primordial wave, sweeping away all reason, releasing a hunger in her that was just as overwhelming.

"Oh, no," she moaned ruefully, but starved for the taste and feel of him, her mouth opened under his, welcoming the thrust of his tongue. Her arms slid up his dripping back to wind themselves tightly around his neck as her body pressed passionately against his.

With a deep groan, Dev staggered back against a huge boulder and pulled her out of the waterfall with him. His mouth still clinging avidly to hers, he slid his legs apart to insure keeping his balance. He propelled her between them, corded thighs gripping hers, taking the length and weight of her trembling body onto his. The way that he was leaning back against the slanted wall of rock, Danielle had the dizzying sensation of lying on top of him as his strong, rough hands moved over her, molding her body to his. She was amazed at how perfectly they fit one another. A molten thrill spread through her as she felt his water-slicked muscles tauten under her, his hardness surging against her.

Danielle dragged her mouth away. "Wait . . ." she gasped, trying to catch her breath. Her heart was pounding against her ribs, louder even than the roar of the waterfall which misted their bodies with every gust of the wind. "Please . . . wait."

"No! I've waited too long for this already," Dev muttered fiercely, though he was just as out of breath as she was. His hands released her body to bury themselves in her wet, tangled hair, drawing her face back to his. "I've been going out of my mind waiting for this," he grated against her mouth before he took her bottom lip between his teeth and sucked it erotically.

Danielle grabbed Dev's shoulders to push him away, just for a moment, just until she could think straight again, only to lose herself in the sleek, warm feel of him.

Sensing her original intention, Dev spun around, reversing their positions, using his gleaming, wet body to block off any chance of escape. The rocky wall Danielle found herself pinned against felt surprisingly good next to her exposed skin, having been worn down to pebble smoothness by the water and warmed by Dev's body heat.

His hands tightened in her hair as he dropped steaming little kisses all over her face and the length of her throat. A shudder tore through her, paralyzing her, when his body slid wetly down hers as he went down on his knees before her. All she could do was cry out as his mouth traced the scoop neck of her maillot with increasingly greedy kisses. She could do nothing at all when his fingers hooked under the narrow straps and pulled the top down to her waist in one convulsive motion.

Danielle gasped soundlessly as a chilly spray of water washed over her bare skin, then loudly as Dev's burning hands swallowed up her breasts.

"Your're even more beautiful than I imagined," he breathed worshipfully, smoky topaz eyes devouring the lush mounds he pressed close together. A tiny pool of water formed instantly between them. Bending his head, he drank it all up.

Shaking uncontrollably, Danielle grabbed Devlin's shoulders to steady herself, hanging on to the sure muscled strength of him by her nails.

With a deep groan of satisfaction, he moved down her breast, his tongue flicking out to catch the drop of water that hung, quivering, on the swollen tip before his mouth closed over it. Her knees buckled under the splintering pleasure his swirling tongue sent spiraling through her. He caught her as her legs gave way and she slid mindlessly down the slippery wall.

The ledge they were kneeling on stretched back to form a cave. Dev pulled her down with him onto the thick, moss-covered floor. "You're so delicious," he rasped against the pulse beating violently in her throat, "you make me want to eat you up." Danielle's fingers bit convulsively into his shoulders, clinging to him as if he were the only fixed point in a universe suddenly spinning out of control. True to his word, he began covering her breasts with devouring little kisses and bites while his hands worked their rough magic on her drenched skin.

Danielle couldn't believe that those wild little moans and cries were coming from *her*, that those were *her* hands pulling him closer, *her* body writhing sensuously against his.

"I knew it would be like this with us," she heard him murmur thickly, joyously, before his mouth moved back up to brush her wet, parted lips. "God, but I want you . . . all of you!" With love-filled eyes, he searched her dazed ones. "Danielle, please . . ." he pleaded hoarsely, "please let me."

A rush of love for him, such as she'd never known, swept over her. A feeling of swelling heat—dense, dark, engulfing—was spreading through her in waves. She physically ached to make him part of her, to take him deep inside her. . . .

"No!" Danielle cried out in sudden panic, pushing against Dev so violently that he fell flat on his back. She scrambled to her feet, barely managing to keep her balance on the slippery ledge before she plunged through the waterfall. Tugging her maillot back into place, she dashed over the moss-covered rocks leading to the foot of the embankment. She stopped only to slip into her sandals and scoop up her wrap; then she ran up the embankment to the trail. And ran, and ran, and ran.

7

Danielle slammed and double-locked the front door behind her, then fell back against it, gasping for breath. She was shaking all over. Even though she'd run the almost half-mile back from the waterfall, she knew that wasn't the reason.

She was filled with shame and self-disgust, a nameless fear. She couldn't believe what she'd just done . . . what she'd been on the verge of doing before Dev stopped to ask her permission, jolting her back to her senses. Never would she have believed herself capable of such abandonment. Maybe Grandmother was right about her after all: sin was bred into her bones, ran in her blood because she was Valmont's bastard daughter. All her life, the fiercely respectable old woman had rubbed Danielle's nose in her shameful heritage at the slightest misbehavior. What would she have said if she'd seen her behaving like an animal with Dev?

Closing her eyes, Danielle let her aching head fall back against the door. For a moment, she actually felt cool, smooth rock against her back instead of wood as her mind was flooded with images and sensations that burned on her face and body, warmed her soul.

No, it hadn't been like that at all. Her still reeling senses wouldn't let her go on lying to herself. Dev's lovemaking had been intense but there had been nothing animalistic about it—or about her response to him. There had been so much love between them. . . .

Pushing violently away from the door, Danielle ran down the hall to her bedroom, leaving a trail of water on the tile floor. Rushing into the adjoining bathroom, she tore a towel off the rack to dry herself with but was pulled up short by the reflection in the mirror over the sink.

Her hair was a streaming black mass flowing wildly over her shoulders. Her eyes were the darkest violet she'd ever seen them. Her swollen lips were red, and her pale skin glowed with a soft, warm flush that no makeup could have matched.

For several minutes Danielle stared back at her image, unable to recognize herself. What was this man doing to her? she wondered in angry confusion.

The sound of fists pounding against the front door startled Danielle out of her thoughts. She clutched the towel fearfully. She'd never expected Dev to come after her. He'd made no attempt to at the waterfall. She was sure that he'd never speak to her again after what she had done to him . . . or was that what she'd been hoping?

"Danielle!" Dev's cry was so loud that it penetrated the closed door and carried down the hall to her bedroom. "Danielle . . . open this door!"

Bending over from the waist, she began drying her hair vigorously, pressing the towel against her ears to block out the sound, but it didn't do much good.

"Let me in . . . Danielle!"

Tearing over to the bedroom door, she slammed it shut, pressing both hands against it to hold it closed as if that would shut out the anguish in Dev's voice. She had expected him to be angry. Although muffled, the frantic sound of his fists banging on the wood felt like blows to her body.

The silence that followed was even worse.

It was just as well, Danielle assured herself a bit desperately; she was glad he was gone. She hoped she'd never see him again. A sudden chill shivered through her. Blaming it on her damp state, she began towel drying her hair again on her way back to the bathroom.

Her mind was a jumble of contradictory thoughts and emotions as she plugged in her blow-dryer. Only one thing was clear—she could no longer delude herself about her feelings for Dev. She loved him. She loved him as she'd never loved anyone in her life—or ever would again.

That mind-boggling admission made Danielle pause, the blow-dryer roaring in one trembling hand, her brush dangling uselessly from the other.

She was sure that, in his way, Dev loved her too—but for how long? How long would it be before he tired of her and his restless artist's soul went chasing after his next "inspiration"? She was not going to end up like her mother. If she let herself love Dev the way that she longed to, the only way that she could—with all of herself and for always—she was asking for sorrow. This man had the power to destroy her. She was not going to end up like her mother!

With grim determination, Danielle resumed blow-drying her hair, struggling to tame its uncharacteristically wild look when the door suddenly flew open and Dev burst into her bedroom.

Still dripping wet, his plastered-down hair emphasized every strong, proud line of his face and heightened the burning intensity of his eyes. The work shirt he'd thrown on without bothering to button it clung damply to his powerful shoulders and back. A sprinkling of water-darkened curls lay flattened against his chest, and his copper skin gleamed. Underneath his jeans, which seemed glued to his legs, the full triangle of his wet bathing suit was clearly visible through the soaked denim.

Once again, Danielle felt that strange quivering, like a wild fluttering of wings, in the pit of her stomach. Why did he have to be so damn beautiful? she wondered miserably.

Thanks to the noise of the blow-dryer she held frozen in midair, Dev spotted her instantly through the open bathroom door. It was the only sound in the room as his intense gaze moved over her body. Danielle suddenly realized that her nylon wrap was clinging tightly to her, emphasizing every curve.

With a determined effort, Dev looked away from her to make a quick survey of the bedroom. He took in the large four-poster bed, the matching armoire and dresser, even the upholstered window seat. It gave Danielle the time she needed to recover and to decide how she was going to deal with him. When Dev looked back over at her, his eyes were expressionless but she could feel the tension in him clear across the room.

"We've got to talk," he stated flatly, closing the bedroom door behind them.

Danielle was about to ask how he managed to get into the house when she remembered the inside stairway to the studio. She never did put a lock on that connecting door. Until that moment, she didn't think she needed one.

"You swore you'd never set foot in this house unless you were invited," she reminded him coolly, trying to get things back to the way they were between them.

"I think we're past that after what just happened," he muttered wryly as he started toward her. "Don't you?"

"No, I don't." As if to prove her point, and not deal with him directly, Danielle went back to drying her hair. "That should never have happened," she added indifferently. They might have been discussing a minor social blunder. "I never meant for that to happen."

"Really? I remember it differently." Leaning against the door jamb, Devlin smiled at her reflection in the mirror, deliberately staring at her kiss-swollen lips. "Are you also going to pretend you don't know what would have happened if I hadn't stopped to ask for your permission?"

Danielle's hand trembled just at the thought but she continued brushing her hair mercilessly, digging the bristles into her scalp. "Don't be so sure," she managed sarcastically. "Just because your caveman approach worked with the other women you've brought there, that doesn't mean . . ."

"Goddammit!" Devlin exploded. "I've never brought another woman there, I told you! Grabbing the nozzle, he pulled the dryer out of her hand and its plug out of the socket—all in one angry motion.

Danielle sucked in her breath but was too startled to say or do anything. She'd forgotten how close to the surface his emotions ran, how intensely he felt and expressed them.

"I won't let you do this to me, Danielle," he bit out. "Scream, yell, throw something at me but don't freeze me out like this!" Turning in the doorway, he tossed the blow-dryer onto the bed. "You know I can't take it when you shut me out," he added miserably.

"Dev, I told you, right from the start, that there could be nothing between us." Brushing her hair away from her face, Danielle started twisting it into a neat coil at the nape of her neck. "And you agreed."

"I would have agreed to anything just to get the chance to be near you," he admitted. "But there is something between us now . . . just as I always knew there would be." A triumphant smile flickered across his face. "Something neither of us can do anything about."

The satisfaction in his tone, the fact that he'd deliberately planned to entrap her infuriated Danielle. "Maybe *you* can't do anything about it," she said caustically, "but *I* can."

"Can you?" His temper flared again as his hands shot out to grip her waist and turn her away from the mirror to face him. "OK, show me," he gritted, pulling her against the long, taut length of his body as his mouth came down hard on hers.

Pushing her hands against his sides, Danielle struggled to twist out of his grasp, away from his ravenous mouth, but his arms locked around her. The pins slid out of her hair and the neat coil unraveled; her hair spilled down over her shoulders.

She was stunned by the intensity of the emotions tearing through her. It was as if he'd pushed a button, wiping out the last half hour, and they picked up exactly where they left off. Waves of dense, dark heat started to engulf her again as her mouth and body melted into his.

"My God, you shake all over when I kiss you," he grated almost angrily. "Why are you doing this to us?"

"Dev, please," Danielle begged desperately, tears filling her eyes. "Please leave me alone."

"No, I won't leave you alone," he muttered fiercely. "I love you too damn much to leave you alone." He buried his hands in the wild mass of her hair, holding her face a breath away from his. "I could understand it if you didn't want me . . . or if I'd done something to make you afraid to trust me. But to deny me because of this absurd prejudice you have against artists . . ." His voice was raw with frustration and his hands released her to fall, in clenched fists, at his sides. "What the hell do you know about artists anyway?"

"Just about all there is to know because I had the best

possible teacher," Danielle blurted out bitterly. "Valmont was my father."

"What?"

"So nobody has to tell me what it's like being in love with an artist because I was there. I saw what it did to my mother." Fighting to hold back tears, she swept past him into the bedroom.

"Valmont was your . . . father?" Dev turned to look over at her from the doorway. "Why didn't you tell me this before?"

"It's not something I'm particularly proud of."

Stepping into the bedroom, he covered the distance between them in a few long strides. "Is that why you kept your married name?"

"No." Too ashamed to face him, Danielle turned her back and stared, unseeing, out the window. "Adams is my maiden name . . . and my mother's since Valmont never bothered to marry her." She was amazed that after all these years it still hurt her to talk about it.

"Being illegitimate is nothing to be ashamed of." Taking her arm gently, Dev turned her toward him. "Danielle, there are no illegitimate children . . . only illegitimate parents."

"That sounds great in theory. But it doesn't work too well in practice. Not when you're a child and all the other kids in school point you out like you're some kind of freak, or make fun of you behind your back. And you'll never know what that meant to someone as sensitive as my mother." With a heavy sigh, Danielle sank down onto the window seat. "It wasn't fashionable to have an illegitimate child in those days. My mother never got over the shame and humiliation." She pulled her legs up onto the window seat and leaned back. "Her superstraitlaced family never let her forget it either, when she was forced to go back to them because Valmont left her for the latest model he was having an affair with—whom he did marry."

"Do you mean Maggie?" he asked, incredulously. "Maggie Carson?"

"Yes." Danielle turned her face away to stare out the window again so he wouldn't see her blinking back the tears. "That was the final blow. My mother had a nervous breakdown. She's been in and out of mental hospitals ever since."

"Jesus," he muttered under his breath.

"And that . . . bastard Valmont never even tried to help her," she cried angrily. "He might have made the difference. No one else was able to help her. Neither the doctors nor Grandmother . . . not even me. And I tried . . . I tried so hard but I couldn't save her. She just kept slipping away, more and more, year after year . . ." Wrapping her arms around her knees, Danielle drew them up to her chest and rested her throbbing forehead on them, a familiar wave of guilt and anger washing over her. *"He was the only one she wanted. But he was too busy becoming a famous artist to care about anybody else!"*

Shaking his head in confusion, Dev leaned against the wall beside the window seat. "I know Valmont was as selfish as a child and totally unreliable, but I'd never have believed he was the kind of man who'd cold-bloodedly turn his back on someone in trouble."

She slanted him a caustic look. "I should have known you'd take his side."

"I'm not taking his side. I just can't reconcile the man I knew with the one you're talking about," he explained patiently. "In spite of all his faults, and he had plenty, he was extravagantly generous—with his time and money, himself even."

"Oh, yes." Danielle laughed bitterly. "Valmont was always very generous with strangers. It was those close to him he had trouble relating to."

Devlin searched her face intently for a moment. "Did he have trouble relating to you too?"

"When Valmont abandoned my mother, he abandoned me also. It was a package deal," she tossed off as she jumped to her feet. The window seat suddenly felt too constricting. She began wandering restlessly around the room. "Not that Grandmother would have allowed him to see me anyway," she was forced to concede, "but if he'd really wanted to, I'm sure he would have found a way."

Danielle shrugged as if it really didn't matter to her one way or the other. "Once he became rich and famous, he did invite me to spend my summer vacations at his villa in the south of France." She stopped in front of the dresser and began compulsively straightening out perfume bottles. "But every year there'd be another wife or mistress . . . sometimes both. The only constant was his drinking. Then, when I was sixteen . . ." She paused and her eyes clouded with the memory. "That was the year my mother went back to the sanatarium for good . . . I started refusing his invitations."

"Was that the last time you saw him? Over ten years ago?"

"Yes. Until . . . I saw him one last time. About five months ago. He just showed up out of nowhere."

Devlin continued studying her intently. "What happened?"

"We had dinner. It was a disaster." Danielle laughed harshly. "He made it pretty obvious that he was disappointed in the way I'd turned out. And I didn't bother to hide my contempt for him and his life-style." She shrugged again, trying to deny the tears stinging her eyes. "It's really not worth talking about."

"I think you should talk about it," Dev insisted softly on his way over to her. "You should let those feelings out instead of keeping them bottled up inside." He placed both hands tenderly on her shoulders and drew her closer. "You've been on the verge of crying ever since you started talking about all this."

"Please don't do that." Her body stiffened defensively as he sought to draw her closer. Part of her wanted nothing more than to let herself sink into the warm, safe circle of his arms, but she knew that she would lose all control if she did.

"Danielle, I just want to help you," he murmured, his eyes tracing the tense lines of her face with loving concern.

"It's not helping," she breathed brokenly. Only with the greatest effort was she able to push herself away from Dev. She began wandering around the room again. Movement seemed to help somehow. "Besides, I never cry." She laughed, but it came out in brittle pieces. "Not even when I was a child. But if I did, I certainly wouldn't waste any tears on Valmont."

"Is *that* who the tears are for?" he asked emphatically.

Danielle wasn't sure what he meant but his question was vaguely disturbing.

"So now you know all about the life and times of Danielle Adams," she said flippantly. "Sorry to have inflicted it on you, but you did ask for it."

"I'm not sorry." He smiled warmly. "I only wish you had told me all this before."

"At least now you know why I'm prejudiced, as you call it, against artists." She stopped in front of him and looked directly up into his face, trying not to notice how beautiful he was. "And why it's . . . impossible for us to be anything but friends."

"I can certainly understand your reasons for being prejudiced now," Dev allowed thoughtfully, choosing to ignore the last part of her statement. "There's just one thing I still can't figure out. If Valmont felt the way you say he did about you, why would he leave his studio to you?"

"Who knows?" Danielle shook her head. It was a question she'd asked herself a few hundred times. "He was always doing crazy things."

"But I know how much the studio meant to him," Dev persisted. "I tried to buy it from him many times. He always refused to sell. I assumed it was because the studio had great personal meaning for him since he did his best work here. But he obviously intended to leave it to you. So he must have loved you . . . in his own way."

"Valmont never loved anyone in his life," Danielle

assured him bitterly. "He seduced everyone in sight but he was incapable of love."

"Did *you* love your father?"

"Me . . . love Valmont?" she asked, astounded.

"Your father," Dev said pointedly.

"He was never my father. He was Valmont." From the skeptical look on Dev's face, Danielle realized that he thought she was deliberately evading the question. "No," she said unhesitatingly. "I hated him. Because of his egotism and his drinking and his womanizing. And especially for what he did to my mother."

"You never had any feelings of love for him at all?" Dev insisted.

"The only thing I . . . admired about him was his creativity," she admitted grudgingly. "He was a great artist. But he had to destroy that, too, like everything else . . . the only thing that I ever loved about him! I can never forgive him for that!"

The silence that followed as Danielle struggled to recover her composure intensified the excruciating embarrassment she felt over her outburst.

"I think you loved your father more than you're willing to admit," Dev said finally. "And, in his way, I think he loved you. There's no other explanation for his leaving his studio to you instead of to one of his legitimate children."

Danielle winced automatically at the word but shrugged it off before she turned and walked away. "Maybe he just felt guilty about neglecting me all those years or . . ." She paused to slant Devlin a sardonic smile over her shoulder. "Or maybe he was playing one last perverse joke on me, since he knew how much I despised his artist's world."

"If you really feel that way, then why did you come to Big Sur?" Dev asked matter-of-factly as he started toward her. "You could have sold the property and kept the money, which would have been considerable." He continued moving toward her in a slow, even casual, way but Danielle had the feeling that he was closing in on her. "Why choose to live here . . . and go to all the trouble of fixing up the place?"

"Well, I . . ."

"I'll tell you why," he interrupted with an irritatingly knowledgeable smile. "Because, whether you like it or not, a part of you is just like your father."

"What?" she snapped, as though he'd insulted her in the worst possible way.

"It's true. You have the same intense love for nature —of anything beautiful. The same eagerness and capacity to enjoy life." He moved even closer and his amber eyes seemed to darken suddenly like the tone of his voice. "And you're unbelievably sensuous. All the things the other part of you—the Adams part— disapproves of, is even afraid of."

"That's ridiculous!" she protested. Unable to handle his disturbing insight, and even more disturbing closeness, she started to turn away but Devlin grabbed her arm, holding her there.

"Danielle, I know exactly what you're going through, believe me," he went on intently, "because it's the same battle I fought with myself for years."

"Let me go," she said coldly though she was beginning to shake inside from the scratchy warmth of his hand on her skin, the closeness of his body.

"I've listened to your side of it." His tone was subdued but firm. "Don't you think it only fair that you listen to my side?"

With an exasperated sigh, Danielle nodded reluctantly. Devlin tugged her over to the bed and, pushing the blow-dryer he'd flung onto it out of the way, sat her down on the edge. Only then did he release her arm.

"Danielle, I *do* understand now why you're so afraid of getting involved with an artist. But your fears are unrealistic because most artists are not like Valmont." He put his hand up to stop her from interrupting as she'd intended. "Let me have my say first, OK? Then you can say what you think." He sighed heavily, running his hand through his thick, still damp hair while he tried to get back on the track. "Valmont was obsessed with acting out that supermacho, self-destructive myth of the Great Artist. But there are plenty of other artists, many living right here in Big Sur, who stay married to one person all their life, have children they care about deeply and just do their work like everybody else."

He paused to make sure that he was getting through to her. She was surprised that it meant so much to him.

"But nobody ever hears about them," he added dryly, "because they don't fit the image of artists which most people find fascinating."

Devlin's words, the tone of his voice, couldn't have been more sincere and Danielle longed to believe him. But he was turning everything she'd always held to be true upside down, leaving her confused and defense-less. "Dev, I . . ."

"Danielle, I'm not like Valmont," he vowed as he sat down next to her on the bed. "I *can* love. I *want* to love . . . you. More than anything else in this world. You've got to believe that." He reached out to cover her hand, which lay clenched and trembling in her lap. "I've never felt so much love for anyone . . . ever. I never will again. You can count on that."

He cupped her chin, tilting her face up to his. He looked deeply into her tear-filled eyes. The depth of emotion she saw reflected in his left her even more shaken. "Such beautiful . . . haunted eyes," he breathed sadly as he dropped a tiny, moist kiss on each eyelid. A tear slid out from under her thick lashes and trickled down her face.

"From the first moment I saw you, I swore I'd be the one to wipe the sadness out of your eyes forever," he murmured against her forehead. His lips felt cool and moist against her burning skin. His throat was barely an inch away from her own lips and she could almost feel the pulse beating violently at its base. Her own pulse began beating erratically, making it impossible for her to think straight, as she inhaled the fresh male scent of him that mingled with the smell of moss which still clung to his skin.

Danielle could feel herself slipping mindlessly away from herself. If she wasn't careful, she would lose herself in him completely—just when she needed to think clearly about everything he'd said to her. Dev's mouth moved eagerly down her face, seeking hers. She pulled back.

The soft glow went out of his eyes, and his expression hardened into hurt anger as he assumed that she was rejecting him again. Releasing her, he jumped to his feet abruptly.

"I love you," he got out with difficulty. "And I understand now why you're doing this to me, but I refuse to go on paying for someone else's sins." He sucked in a long, hard breath and let it out in ragged shreds. "I've tried very hard these last few weeks to prove to you that I'm not like Valmont. But I know now that nothing I can say or do is ever going to convince you. You're too determined to hang onto the only thing you know, the only thing you're comfortable with . . . your fear and hatred!"

Devlin stormed over to the door before Danielle could recover sufficiently to defend herself.

"You accuse Valmont of being incapable of love," he added bitterly before slamming his way out, "but what about you?"

8

Danielle brought her third cup of coffee back to the window seat with her. Through the spotless glass, the morning fog clung tenaciously to the mountains as though unwilling to end its gauzy embrace. She barely noticed how the mist and soft sun melted their rough contours, turning the multihued cliffs and slopes into a Japanese watercolor. Nor did she enjoy the cheerful clamoring of the birds. She was too intent on watching the driveway and listening for the familiar purr of Devlin's XJ-S—when she wasn't checking her watch.

Five to nine.

It was five minutes to nine and Devlin still hadn't arrived. She was beginning to fear that he wouldn't show up at all again. She decided to wait until nine. Then she would definitely go back to work. She couldn't just sit there and mope as she had done the day before.

Dev's final, bitter words had hurt and angered Danielle at first, but they forced her finally to deal with her feelings about him. Unable to throw herself into work, as she always did when something bothered her, she'd spent all of the day before, and half the night, going over their relationship. She'd never denied that she was intensely attracted to Dev from the moment they'd met or that she'd fallen in love with him, in spite of herself. What she'd never admitted to herself, until yesterday, was how much she liked the man. Never in her life had she admired a man so much, or for so many reasons. Just being with him made her happy in a way she'd never known. The thought of never seeing him again was devastating.

The more Danielle went over the events of the last few weeks, questioning her motives, dissecting her responses, the more she realized that Devlin was right. Blinded by fears and hang-ups from her past, she had never treated him fairly. She'd always seen him through the distorting lens of Valmont, never as he really was. But Dev was wrong about one thing: she was not incapable of love. Her love for him filled her to bursting. If only she could find the courage to show it. If only it wasn't too late.

It was ten after nine.

Danielle took several anxious sips of cold coffee. She'd wait until nine-fifteen. Once again, she stifled the urge to phone Dev. She'd called him several times the day before, the last time after midnight, but either he wasn't home or he wasn't answering the phone. Wondering where he might be, and with whom, had helped keep her up half the night and was now churning the coffee around in her stomach.

She swore silently at herself. Devlin was not Valmont, and she was going to have to stop being so suspicious or any chance for a relationship between them would be . . .

The unmistakable purr of the Jaguar's motor cut through Danielle's thoughts but was instantly drowned out by the sudden pounding of her heart as she watched the car gliding around the curve. It got loud again when her heart seemed to stop. Dev was not alone.

His companion was a lovely girl in her early twenties with long black hair and a well-rounded figure. The portfolio she carried, as well as the way she carried herself, proclaimed her to be a professional model.

When they passed the kitchen window, Danielle got a perfunctory nod from Dev and a toothpaste-ad smile from the model. In sheer misery, she watched them mount the stairs to the studio.

Determined not to give in to her naturally distrustful nature so soon after her promise to herself to change, Danielle quickly suppressed her jealousy. Using live models was an essential part of a sculptor's work, she lectured herself as she started to reline the cabinet shelves. Devlin was a sculptor. Valmont might have made a habit of going to bed with his models but Devlin was not Valmont. The fact that Dev worked with nude models was something that she was going to have to learn to accept if they were going to have a loving, mature relationship, she told herself. But she made such a mess of the shelving paper that she had to peel it off the shelf.

When Devlin shared his lunch with the model in the studio, then drove off with her at the end of the day without so much as a word to Danielle, she became convinced that she'd been right about him after all. The way he'd acted toward her during the last two weeks, all his lovely words the other night had been merely attempts to fool her into believing that he was different so that he could get her into bed. He certainly didn't waste any time finding a replacement.

The replacement, however, was replaced herself the next morning by an even lovelier model. *She* lasted only two days. A record, as it turned out, because for the next week and a half, Danielle watched in confused amazement from her window seat as a different model drove up every morning. They were all quite cheerful on arrival and rather despondent on departure, which, with every passing day, was getting earlier and earlier.

As miserable as Danielle felt about Dev's deliberately ignoring her and his continuing to have lunch upstairs with the model of the day, she couldn't help being curious. She'd never heard so much pacing about overhead. Those ceiling-shaking footsteps could only belong to Dev. She would have given anything to be a fly on the studio wall just to find out what was going on up there.

Then, one afternoon, before the latest model had finished backing her convertible out of the driveway,

Danielle heard a loud crash overhead, followed by an even more frightening silence.

All Danielle could think about as she went running upstairs to the studio were the huge blocks of marble she'd seen suspended on pulleys from the ceiling. All she cared about was making sure Dev wasn't hurt.

She didn't realize how much she cared until the painful constriction in her chest eased, allowing her to breathe again, once she caught sight of him. But her relief was momentary.

Dev was frantically tearing all his carefully drawn sketches off the cork wall and ripping them apart. The jagged pieces floated down over the large clay-stand he'd obviously knocked over before. Lumps of wet clay covered the floor around his feet. When there was nothing left to tear up, he stalked over to the modeling stand that held the four-foot statue which had evolved from those sketches—the one he'd been working on for almost two weeks.

Stunned by the look of anguish on his face, Danielle remained frozen in the doorway, unable to say or do anything. Still unaware of her presence, Dev clenched his hands into fists as he glared at the sculpture.

Even in its unfinished state it was beautiful. The vibrant sensuality and raw emotion which characterized all his work were already evident in every line of the nude lovers' bodies.

The reclining woman, all softly yielding curves, had been captured at the moment of loving surrender. The figure of the man kneeling at her feet was only roughed out but desire already tautened the powerful muscles in his back as he bent over her. A kind of adoration, expressed by the way he reached out for her yet seemed too awed to touch her, stayed his lips as he was about to kiss the hollow between her breasts.

As if Devlin couldn't bear to look at the statue any longer, he suddenly raised his clenched fists over it. "Dev . . . no!" Danielle cried out before he could bring them crashing down on the statue. "What are you doing?" She went rushing over to him. "Why?"

"Because it's no damn good," he muttered once he recovered from the shock of her being there, his still-clenched fists at his sides. "That's why."

"But it's so beautiful!"

He smiled bitterly. "How would you know?" For a moment, Danielle wasn't sure whether he was referring to the artistic merits of the sculpture or the passion it depicted so evocatively. "You always said you didn't know anything about art and couldn't care less."

"Well, I care about this and I won't let you destroy it," she blurted out, surprising them both. Dev slowly unclenched his fists and took a step toward her. Danielle stepped back, reacting automatically to the unnerving effect his being close always had on her. "I don't . . . understand . . ." She motioned toward the statue. "What's wrong with it?"

"Everything that's wrong with us, that's what's wrong with it," he muttered, frustration edging his tone. "It keeps getting in my way, I . . . I can't work anymore. It's like a . . . a mental block. No matter how hard I try to concentrate . . . knowing that you're just downstairs, I . . ." He took another step toward her as though drawn to her in spite of himself, his eyes searching her face intently. He hadn't looked at her with such longing since the last time they were alone when he'd wanted to make love to her.

It had exactly the same effect on Danielle, thrilling and frightening her at the same time. "But I . . . I've tried not to make any unnecessary noise. I didn't mean to bother you."

The soft glow in Dev's eyes went out. His face hardened uncharacteristically. "How very thoughtful of you," he murmured sarcastically before turning away from her to stride angrily over to where the clay-stand still lay overturned on the floor.

Danielle could have kicked herself. She had known exactly what he meant. Why had she wanted him to think that she hadn't? Was it because she found it impossible to believe? Valmont certainly would never have allowed a woman to interfere with his work. . . .

Damn, she thought, she was doing it again, judging Dev by Valmont's code of behavior. Kneeling down, she began picking up the torn sketches. "Dev, I didn't mean to . . ."

"Forget it." He cut off her attempt at an apology as he finished righting the heavy wooden stand. "You know how temperamental we 'crazy' artists are."

Dev's bitter sarcasm hurt Danielle even more because she knew it was so unlike him. Normally, he had such a warm and outgoing personality. She blamed herself for the change in him. If only there was something she could say or do. Suddenly noticing that the sketches she'd been collecting into a neat pile had been ripped mostly in half, she started trying, somewhat compulsively, to put them back together again.

"Besides, it's my own damn fault," Dev muttered in disgust. Keeping his back to her, he began scooping the lumps of modeling clay off the floor and dumping them back on the stand. "I should have known it was no good once the . . . inspiration for it was . . . ruined. But I'd already done the sketches, and I was more excited about them than I'd been about anything in a long time so . . ." He sighed heavily. All the pain and frustration he'd been hiding from her these last weeks was in it. But he seemed unable to stop himself now that it was finally coming out in the open. "Anyway, I figured with another model . . . and some imagination I'd still be able to make it work, but I was wrong about that too."

Danielle had finished reassembling the charcoal drawings, which she'd spread out in front of her on the floor. She stared at them in amazement. They were variations of the same pose, but the woman's face in all of them was her own. What amazed her was that *this* was how Dev saw her—beautiful, loving and sensuous.

"What are you doing?" Wiping his hands on the wet sponge he always kept next to the statue, Dev slanted her a perplexed look.

Danielle didn't look up at him because he would have seen the tears she was blinking back. "Have you got any, uhh . . . Scotch tape?"

"Scotch tape? What for?"

"I'm sure we can save these sketches. I've gotten most of them back together."

"Don't bother," he said with a defeated shrug as he stepped over to her. "I'm just going to throw them all out."

"Why? Just give me some Scotch tape. I know I can fix them so . . ."

"Forget it," he muttered disgustedly and went down on one knee beside her. "It's no use." He reached for the sketches impatiently, almost angrily.

"No!" Danielle blocked him with her arm to keep him from getting at them. She didn't know why they meant so much to her, only that they did, and that it was all tied up with their relationship somehow. "I can fix them! Then you can finish the statue, once you find the right model."

"It's no use! Why can't I make you understand that? I've tried for almost two weeks to find the 'right' model—but they're just faces and bodies that don't mean a damn thing to me! *This* . . ." Reaching under her arm, Devlin grabbed part of a sketch, one with his image of Danielle on it, and practically shook it in her face. *"This* is what I'm trying to recreate . . . what I see when I look at you . . . what only you can make me feel! Because *that's* what the goddamn statue's all about . . . and *that's* why I can't finish it!"

Danielle was totally stunned. She could see that Devlin was waiting anxiously for some response to his emotional outburst but she was shaking so much inside that she could barely breathe.

Crumbling the drawing up in his fist, Devlin rose slowly to his feet. "I'm sure you think that's 'crazy' too." His face and tone were now empty of emotion, his body rigid from the effort. Only his hand, which continued crushing the sketch, gave him away.

"No, I . . ."

"You're probably right," Devlin cut her off sarcastically, tossing the balled-up sketch in her lap before he turned and walked away from her. "There probably is a kind of madness in trying to create in art what you know you can't have in life." He paused thoughtfully in front of his unfinished statue of the lovers. "Maybe that's why I wanted this to be everything I dreamed it could have been with us . . . instead of this lump of lifeless . . . impotent clay!"

Danielle could feel the frustration building up in him again. It was almost palpable. She realized now that it was because of her but she was afraid that he might try to take it out on the statue again.

"Dev, *I'm* the one with the screwed-up notions . . . not you." Jumping to her feet, she rushed over to him. "I've been so wrong . . . about so many things . . . especially about you."

Danielle's halting admission was made as much to herself as to Dev. She felt too ashamed to look at him. Tears misted her violet eyes as she contemplated the emotion-charged sculpture.

"And this statue isn't *your* 'mad' dream. Everybody dreams of finding a love . . . like this, but most of us don't know . . . or can't believe that it exists." Unable to stop herself, Danielle reached out to touch the male lover's worshipful face. "You've got to show them that it does exist . . . and how beautiful it can be." Her fingers glided down the desire-tautened muscles in his back.

She was surprised at the texture of the clay—it had the cool, sleek feel of damp flesh.

Suddenly aware of what she was doing, Danielle pulled her hand away. It started fiddling with the oversized metal tab on her zipper when she forced herself to look up at Devlin. "That's why you've got to finish the statue."

Devlin shook his head wearily, as though he'd given up trying to explain it to her. "I can't do it."

"Yes, you can." Danielle smiled encouragingly. "Come on." With one quick, determined motion, she unzipped the front of her jumpsuit. "Let's go to work."

"Huh?"

She caught a glimpse of Dev's startled expression as she brushed quickly past him. She had to keep moving. She couldn't stop to think about what she was doing or she'd never be able to go through with it. "It can't be much later than two o'clock." Stepping out of her jumpsuit, she kicked it to one side. Her sandals followed. "There's hours of light left," she rattled on. Somehow she couldn't stop talking either. "We should be able to get quite a bit of work done." Unhooking her bra, she dropped it on the denim pile by her feet.

Danielle's movements were deliberately brisk, efficient—until she got to her panties. She hesitated. But only for a moment. She couldn't hold back on him now. It had to be everything or nothing.

She slid her panties down and shivered involuntarily. She hadn't realized how cold her hands were. Her face was burning. Stepping out of her panties, her foot got tangled in the silky fabric and she tripped slightly.

Mentally cursing herself for a klutz, she made her way resolutely, if somewhat shakily, over to the bed.

"I assume that's where you want me to pose," she said, cringing inside even as she said it. Why else would the bed be up on the model's platform? But why didn't *he* say something for a change? Except for a sharp intake of breath when she'd started undressing, Devlin hadn't uttered a sound. Since Danielle wasn't able to face him, she had no idea what he was thinking or feeling.

As always, even with her back to him, she was disturbingly aware of his presence. She could have pinpointed the exact spot he was standing on though she couldn't have guessed that he was standing there as if nailed to the floor. But she knew how intently he was watching her. She could feel his gaze on her skin like a caress.

Danielle's legs were shaking so much when she stepped onto the platform that she was afraid that she might trip again. She wasn't sure which she was more nervous about, being naked in front of him or his being disappointed in her body. But she knew that this was the moment of truth. She couldn't put off facing Dev any longer.

Drawing in a long, ragged breath, she spun completely around and plopped herself down on the edge of the bed. Bending her head, she began pulling out the hairpins which held her chignon in place. "I assume you want me to let my hair down . . . I mean, like the woman in the statue?"

"Yes . . . please." Devlin's hoarse reply barely carried over to her though he was standing only a few feet away.

"I really hope I can be of help to you," she rattled on, "even though I've never done this . . . kind of thing before." Dropping the last hairpin on the carpet, Danielle shook her head, sending her thick black hair cascading over her bare shoulders.

She started smoothing out the perfectly smooth sheet which covered the bed. "I'm not quite sure what to do . . . so you're going to have to tell me what you want." Why did everything she said sound suggestive? Reaching for the pillow, she began fluffing it up vigorously.

"You don't have to do anything," Devlin assured her softly. "Just be yourself." He was aware of how difficult this was for her and was oddly moved by it. Sensing that she couldn't bring herself to lie down on the bed with him watching and that she was rapidly running out of things to fluff up or smooth out, he turned his attention to the statue.

"Just try to relax," he continued in a calm, soothing tone which reminded her of her dentist, "and make yourself as comfortable as you can." Loosening the clamp that held the top armature in place, Dev swung the male figure out to one side, which gave him clear access to the female figure. Danielle noticed that, despite his precise movements and outward composure, his hands were shaking when he secured the clamp again.

A rush of love and tenderness went through her. Tossing the fluffed-up pillow back in place, she stretched out on the bed. She was still feeling a bit self-conscious so she was surprised at how naturally her body fell into the pose.

"That's pretty good." Devlin stepped up onto the platform and smiled warmly. "Are you absolutely sure you've never done this kind of thing before?" he teased while he began making adjustments in the pose. "I'd say you were a natural."

Danielle realized that Dev's bantering tone was meant to help her relax under his touch, but she had the feeling that he needed to joke about the potentially explosive situation in order to defuse it for himself as well. His strong, sensitive fingers touched her as lightly and briefly as possible while he adjusted her arms and legs, respositioned her hips, but she could feel his suppressed tension right through her skin. It set off a quivering in back of her knees and deep in the pit of her stomach.

"Who knows? You may have a whole new career ahead of you." Hunkering down at the head of the bed, Devlin began arranging Danielle's hair so that part of it spilled over her shoulders onto her full, rounded breasts while the rest tumbled over the pillow in disarray. His face was so close to hers she could feel his warm, uneven breath brushing her temple.

She hadn't realized that she was holding her breath until she released it in ragged shreds after Dev sprang to his feet and off the platform in one agile motion. Danielle's dazed eyes followed him back to the statue, taking in the strong, beautiful lines of his body, the vibrant way that he moved. The realization of how much she'd missed him was a physical ache inside her.

Expertly working some clay in one large hand to

make sure that its consistency was still right, Dev turned to view Danielle fully from the new perspective. His amber eyes glowed with love as they held hers. He made no attempt to hide his feelings now that he was at a safe distance. "Thank you." His voice was husky with emotion, his face all naked feeling. "You don't know what this means to me."

Once again, Danielle was at a loss as to how to respond. She'd never known a man, especially one as strong and virile as he was, to show his feelings so unashamedly. The aching for him intensified.

Before she could recover enough to reply, Dev turned his attention back to the statue. When he looked over at her again, it was with the clear, probing eyes of a sculptor as he set to work finishing the statue.

Danielle tensed up at first but soon found herself too fascinated to be self-conscious. She realized now why the bed was up on the platform; it was so that the model would be at eye level with the statue, but it also allowed her to watch his every move.

She was surprised that he didn't use any instruments, only his strong fingers. She marveled at their dexterity and power. They seemed to have a life of their own, to be directed by some deep, instinctive feeling rather than by conscious well as they applied the clay in sure, broad strokes, building in layers, from the inside out. She could see the statue coming alive before her eyes and was amazed that Dev was able to create such a feeling of life out of lifeless matter.

For the first time Danielle understood, on a purely gut level, what it meant to be an artist. And she felt herself being drawn irresistibly into the creative, almost sexual energy that he projected so intensely. It was like an electric current flowing between them, binding them in some mysterious way.

She was only vaguely aware of the sun streaming through the skylight overhead, warming her skin, or how comfortable the mattress was now that her body had relaxed into it. Dev's probing eyes had a mesmerizing effect on her. They seemed determined to see beyond the physical boundary of skin into the deepest, most secret part of her.

Danielle found herself opening up, no longer able to hide the love and desire for him that was aching inside her. It showed in her eyes and moistly parted lips, in an unconscious softening of her body.

What Dev's searching eyes had uncovered, his hands translated into pure emotion. Caught up in the very feelings that he'd aroused, Dev expressed his own love and longing for Danielle, caressing every line and curve of the nude figure as though he were touching her. With exquisite tenderness, he began smoothing the clay to give it the texture of flesh. Danielle shivered as his thumb moved over the rounded curve of a hip with long, sensuous strokes, and when it glided along the soft undercurve of a breast, her own breasts began to tingle.

Dev's sharp intake of breath shattered the spell she'd been caught up in. Following his frozen stare, she realized that her nipples had grown taut with excitement. A deep flush spread up from her breasts over her neck and face. When she was able to look over at Dev again, he'd already covered the distance between them and was springing up onto the platform.

Only the greatest effort of will stopped him, held him at the foot of the bed, tightening every muscle of his powerful body as his golden eyes pleaded for her permission.

"Yes," Danielle breathed unhesitatingly, "oh, yes."

With a grateful sigh, Devlin started toward her only to stop himself again as though he'd just remembered something. "Damn!" Tearing off his tank top, he began wiping his clay-smudged hands on it. "*This* isn't how I wanted it to be." His sweeping gesture with the tank top took in the stark surroundings, the single bed, finally himself before he tossed it aside. "I've wanted you so much . . ." His gaze, no longer the objective one of a sculptor, moved hungrily over every inch of her. "But not like . . . this." He came over to her anyway. He couldn't have stopped himself now even if he had wanted to.

Danielle was long past stopping herself, but Devlin's unexpected vulnerability melted the last lingering traces of doubt and fear.

With a heavy sigh, he sank down on the edge of the bed next to her, the rough denim of his jeans scratching her thigh. "I wanted it to be special," he explained ruefully, touching something deep inside her. He raked an impatient hand through his shaggy hair, then rubbed the light stubble on his chin, which to her only added to the rugged beauty of his face. "I need a shave . . . and I'm all sweaty and . . ."

"Oh, Dev . . ." Danielle didn't know whether to laugh or to cry. "There's no soap or cologne in this world that smells as good as you." Sitting up impulsively, she buried her face in the damp, silky hair on his chest and breathed him in deeply. "Nothing in this whole world smells as good as you do."

With a strangled groan, Devlin sank both hands in her hair, drawing her face up to his until they were barely a breath apart. "I just wanted to make it beautiful for you," he whispered raggedly before his mouth took hers with a fierce tenderness.

Danielle could have told him that his kiss was the most achingly beautiful sensation she'd ever known but she didn't want it to end. Neither, it seemed, did he. Her fingers dug into the moist silk of his chest hair and she felt the sexual urgency which tautened his powerful muscles. Yet his mouth continued to move tenderly on hers as he kissed her over and over again, long, languorous kisses that seemed to go on forever.

Shaking, out of breath, Danielle dragged her mouth away. Dev's fingers uncoiled in her hair, releasing her. Her head fell back, exposing the delicate curve of her throat. He bent to kiss the pulse beating wildly at its base, allowing her several gasps of desperately needed air.

His arms locked around her and hers went up to wrap themselves around his neck as he crushed her to him. The same shudder went through both of them at the sudden burning contact of skin on skin and they shared the same moan.

"God, but I want you," Dev ground out passionately on her mouth, "all of you . . . now." He released her suddenly and she slid out of his arms to fall back onto the bed. Jumping to his feet, he quickly unzipped his jeans and pushed them down to his hips—where they got stuck. "Damn, why do they make these things so tight?" he muttered, working them carefully past the source of his problem.

Laughter bubbled up inside Danielle and she couldn't keep it from spilling over.

"Are you laughing at me? First you get me in this state and then you make fun of me." He gave her a mock frown as his shorts followed his jeans to the floor. "I'll get you for that."

The laughter caught in her throat but it wasn't because of his joking threat. The sheer power and beauty of his masculinity awed her. The sun streaming through the skylight burnished his copper skin, high-lighting every muscle of his perfectly proportioned body. It turned his lion's mane of hair and the tawny sprinkling on his chest and limbs into gold, dazzling her. Though Danielle knew that the sight of this man would be imprinted on her brain forever, she suddenly wished she were an artist so that she could capture and immortalize such vibrant beauty.

Dev was too busy making love to Danielle with his own eyes to notice her reaction as he moved swiftly back to the bed. "And to think I've got a king-size bed at home that's been dying for the feel of you," he teased, easing the long, hard length of his body down alongside her. The single bed was so narrow that he was forced to lie on his side. His feet hung out over the end.

Turning onto her side, Danielle slid over to the edge of the bed to make room for him. "No, don't," he protested thickly. One arm reached out to circle her shoulders, pulling her close, while the other molded the front of her body to his. "This may not be as bad as I thought." He laughed, his eyes darkening to the color of smoky topaz before his mouth came down on hers hungrily. Danielle surged passionately against him as his burning hand glided slowly down her back, all the way to her thighs and back up again. Then down again.

"You're so soft," he groaned, "so unbelievably soft." His teeth nipped the corner of her trembling lips as his hand continued moving over her with long, sensuous strokes.

She was astonished at the pleasure he found in touching her and gasped at the tingling fire his sandpapery fingers trailed on her skin. She never would have believed that the mere act of touching could be so erotic, and she felt herself coming vibrantly alive under the hand which molded her like clay.

With a growing urgency, Devlin pushed her down onto her back, burying his face between her breasts as he filled both hands with her. While his mouth roamed from one to the other, Danielle arched into him, sinking her fingers into the tawny thickness of his hair to press him closer still. With eager hands, teeth and tongue Dev loved, not only the swollen tips, but every part of her breasts.

"God, but I love the feel of you," he groaned against her skin as he brushed his face back and forth over her breasts with a kind of rapture. His scratchy stubble added to the pleasure she felt when he rubbed his cheek all over the softly rounded curve of her belly, his mouth leaving warm, wet traces on her skin until it sought and found the most sensitive, secret part of her.

Danielle gasped in shock, but her body arched to meet him as he loved her in a way she'd never known, in the most intimate way possible. The very intimacy of it frightened her. She'd never felt so vulnerable or exposed. She cried out, but her cry was a mixture of fear and pleasure at the intensity of the unaccustomed sensations that went spiraling through her.

Devlin reached up to touch Danielle's clenched fingers, which she hadn't realized she'd been biting. "I didn't hurt you?"

"No . . ." She gasped for air. "No, it's . . . so much . . . too much." Her arms reached out for him, longing to make him part of her. Only he could free her of the exquisite ache still coiling inside her. "Please," she begged. "I can't take anymore."

"But there's going to be more," Dev vowed thickly. He lifted himself up over her and, placing his hands on either side of her shoulders, rested his weight on them. The long, firm length of his body hung poised over hers. "I want to give you more."

Something inside her quivered at his words and she marveled at his control. Dev lowered himself slowly on top of her and she felt the violent pounding of his heart, the tremors coursing through his body. She wrapped her arms and legs around him as she went all open to him. She cried out again when he entered her, and so did he. But he didn't move. Except to bring his lips to within a breath of hers.

"Can you feel me?" he breathed. "I want you to feel me . . . all of me . . . just as I want to feel all of you." His arms tightened around her and his body crushed hers deeper into the bed. *"Do you?"*

"Oh, my God . . . yes!" she gasped. How could she not feel him? Every part of him was touching every part of her. He was a raging in her blood. A throbbing deep inside her, sending ever-widening circles of pleasure rippling through her. He was all that was left of reality.

Danielle couldn't have said when the slow, tantalizingly drawn-out movement began, or who began it, because they moved as one. She'd never known that two people could fit one another so perfectly, fusing completely together. Or that a man could want to give a woman so much. A rush of love, so intense it was physical, welled up inside her as her arms tightened around him, her body arching into his.

The hard groan that tore from Dev's throat and the shudder that convulsed him intensified the excitement that Danielle found in giving him as much pleasure as he gave her, though she was amazed that she could do this to him. With each deepening thrust she could feel herself starting to come apart, piece by piece. Soon there would be nothing left of her, but she wasn't afraid anymore. She longed to lose herself completely in this man who was giving her all of himself, filling her with so much love. Convulsively, her nails dug into the powerful muscles contracting in his back, urging him closer, deeper. His cry of ecstasy filled her with a joy and power she'd never known and then she was disintegrating, dissolving utterly, melting into him.

9

~~~~~~~~~~~~~~

"Having second thoughts?" Devlin asked as he smoothly executed the turn off Monte Verde Street onto Ocean Avenue, leaving city hall behind.

Danielle hadn't realized that she'd been staring out the car window, lost in thought. "What?"

"Traditionally, it's the man who's supposed to have second thoughts after taking out a marriage license," he teased, but she thought she detected a slight strain in his tone.

"No, of course not." With a loving smile, she placed a reassuring hand on his thigh. The muscles under his navy slacks reacted instantly to her touch. "I was just . . . daydreaming, I guess."

"Looked like a pretty serious daydream." He slid her a wry glance. "Did you talk to your grandmother this morning? You've got that . . . look."

Danielle was amazed at how well he read her after only two months together. "Yes, I did."

"What did she say about our getting married next week?" He swerved to avoid hitting the Monterey pine standing in the center of the parkway.

Danielle laughed lightly, taking advantage of the opportunity to change the subject. "I don't think I'll ever get used to seeing trees growing smack in the middle of the street because there's a law against cutting them down here, or to the absence of traffic lights in Carmel . . . and parking meters." She looked out the side window again, concentrating on the variety of boutiques lining the town's pine-shaded main street and the dwellings that flanked the unpaved residential streets which meandered through a profusion of flowers and shrubs.

The houses, each built to suit the individual taste of its owner, were an eclectic assortment of Old English, Spanish adobe and Hansel-and-Gretel architecture. The droll, dollhouse structures, snuggling among the gnarled cypresses and pines, added to the storybook look of a forest village encircled by mountains and rolling hills.

"Was your grandmother very upset because we're keeping the wedding an intimate affair?" Devlin asked in that tone of voice that Danielle had learned was deceptively casual.

"No, I . . ." She sighed nervously. It had been difficult enough telling her grandmother that she'd broken her engagement to Howard and that she wouldn't be going back to Boston now that the summer was over. "I didn't really tell her."

In the awkward silence that followed, Danielle felt the sudden tension in Dev's thigh. "Why not?"

"I didn't get the chance. I was dressing when she called and I was already late for our appointment." She squeezed his thigh reassuringly again, enjoying the feel of his strong muscles and their unconscious reaction to her touch. "I'll call her back tonight."

Devlin chuckled with perverse satisfaction. "I wonder what she would have said if she had seen you in that outfit." His eyes skimmed over her scoop necked, off-the-shoulder Mexican blouse and matching embroidered skirt. The exquisite Indian jewelry that he'd given her as an engagement present circled her neck and dangled from her newly pierced ears. She wore her hair loose, as she always did when she was with Dev now, and it framed her tanned face, cascading over her bare, golden-brown shoulders. "You look beautiful," he murmured thickly.

"Thank you." She pushed a stray lock of hair behind her ear self-consciously. As much as it pleased her, she was still amazed that he found her beautiful. "But I don't think Grandmother would agree."

In fact, Danielle was sure that her grandmother wouldn't have approved of any of the changes that she'd undergone these last two months. Danielle herself was astonished at the difference in her since she and Devlin had become lovers.

Dev's love had gradually demolished the defensive wall she'd built around herself. The more she opened herself up to him and was rewarded with love instead of the rejection or criticism she was accustomed to—even anticipated—the easier it became. For the first time since she was forced to leave Big Sur as a child, Danielle felt as though she belonged, that she wasn't just being put up with but was truly loved and wanted.

As though aware of her insecurity, Devlin went out of his way to make her feel a part of his world. Several nights a week, he gave small dinner parties to introduce her to his friends in the artists' colony. She was fully aware that most of the couples they entertained were married and had children and that some of them had been married for many years. It was obviously Dev's sly way of proving to her that she had been wrong about artists, while showing her the kind of life they would share if she agreed to marry him. As incredible as it would have seemed to Danielle two months before, she had come to believe that they could have a wonderful life together.

Yet, every now and then, that nameless fear which had haunted her all her life would hit her. It came from out of nowhere, usually when she was her happiest—like today.

"That sure looks like a heavy daydream," Dev commented dryly as he completed the turn onto Dolores Street where the Valmont Art Gallery, though only two stories high like the rest of the buildings in Carmel, managed to dominate the other art galleries and boutiques lining both sides of the street.

"I'm sorry." She shook her head. "I don't know what's the matter with me today."

"You're not anxious about meeting Maggie Carson, are you?" he asked with genuine concern while maneuvering the XJ-S down the cobblestone alley to the parking lot in back.

"I don't know." Danielle shrugged uncomprehendingly. The two women had managed to get through the entire summer without meeting face to face. Important business matters had been conducted over the telephone. But, as much as she'd have preferred to, she couldn't give Maggie Carson her decision about the art gallery over the phone. Danielle felt sure that the woman who had taken Valmont away from her mother would be upset enough as it was.

"Maybe that's what it is," Danielle agreed when she accepted Dev's hand to help her out of the car.

He shut the door behind her but, instead of releasing her hand, he swallowed it up in his. "Remember this place?"

"I sure do."

"Right . . . here," he murmured, pulling her close, "on this very spot is where I kissed you the first time." Bending his head, he brushed her lips softly with his. "Remember?"

"I don't think I'll ever forget it." Danielle's hand went up, gliding past his blazer, to play with the tawny curls peeking out from the open collar of his sport shirt. She gave them a hard little tug. "Or what you put me through . . . chasing me all over the lot."

"Did I? I guess I did." He smiled sheepishly as his arms went around her, holding her lightly. "I was frantic. All I knew was that I had to see you again. I couldn't let you just walk out of my life." His lips brushed hers again— slowly, more erotically this time, sending tiny shivers all through her. "You're not sorry, are you?"

"Oh, no," she moaned, "no."

Devlin tilted his head back and looked into her eyes searchingly. "You're not sorry you agreed to marry me? I know I've been pressuring you these last few weeks, but I was afraid that with the end of the summer, you might go back to Boston and . . ." His voice trailed off as the thought of her leaving him made it impossible for him to go on.

"Oh, Dev. I couldn't leave you even when I wanted to." Winding her arms around his neck, Danielle pressed her body closer to his, trying to wipe out the doubts her behavior in the car had obviously awakened in him. Her lips parted in anticipation of his kiss. Although she'd expected it, she was stunned, as she always was, by the intensity of it. His arms tightened around her, pulling her into the tautening heat of him as his mouth moved on hers with that passionate hunger that she always found so exciting. Her body melted mindlessly into his.

"I would never have let you go," Dev grated against her cheek when he finally dragged his mouth away. "I would have chased you over every parking lot in Boston." He laughed and the happy, confident sound of it pleased her. "Right now, I'd rather be chasing you around the bedroom," he added thickly as his hands slid down her back to press her hips against his so she could feel for herself how much he wanted her.

"Dev . . . lin!" Danielle gasped, pushing away from him. But her sparkling eyes and barely suppressed smile made it clear that she wasn't as shocked as she pretended to be. "You're . . . impossible!"

"*Me* impossible?" he countered with mock indignation. "*You're* the one who brings out the monster in me . . . no pun intended." He thrust both hands deep into his pants pockets as Danielle burst out laughing.

"Come on, let's get this damn business over with," he muttered. Sliding one arm around her shoulders, he tugged her along with him as he started toward the entrance. "Afterward, I'm going to take you to the classiest restaurant in Big Sur for dinner so we can celebrate our marriage license and then . . ." He hugged her shoulders, pulling her closer as they ascended the wobbly wooden steps. "Then I'm going to take you home and I'm going to make love to you like nobody, not even me, has ever made love to you."

"Dev . . . lin!"

"Unless you'd rather go to a movie," he teased, holding the door open for her.

"No, I like your first idea better . . . as long as I get equal time." Her smile was full of mischief, like that of a child excited by her own daring. "There are a few things I've been wanting to do to you too."

"Christ," he groaned, "don't say that. I just got myself back to where I'm presentable again."

She laughed happily as she sailed through the doorway. "You'll just have to keep your hands in your pockets."

Danielle's heart was as light as her step when she moved quickly down the hall with Devlin. It occurred to her that she'd never felt so young or carefree. Stopping at the arched entrance to the main gallery, where a retrospective of postimpressionist paintings was on display, she scanned the faces of the twenty or so tourists milling about.

"I just realized that I don't even know what Maggie

Carson looks like." Danielle froze as she spotted a face that she did know and watched as the masklike perfection of it was broken by a radiantly excited smile.

"Dev, darling . . . finally!" Valerie Sheldon hurried over to them as quickly as her four-inch heels would allow. "I've been waiting for you for over an hour."

"Hi, Valerie. How've you been?"

Valerie Sheldon ignored Devlin's outstretched hand to embrace him, kissing him effusively on both cheeks. Danielle suppressed the urge to hit her.

"Where's Lyle?" Dev asked after managing to extricate himself.

"Lyle?" Her pale gray eyes widened as it took her a moment to recollect her husband. She was wearing skintight designer jeans and a punk-style tee shirt with strategically placed cutouts which allowed tantalizing glimpses of her unconfined breasts. The motorcyle chain belt, slung low on her lean hips, matched the thick slave bracelets circling both wrists. The outfit should have looked ridiculous on a woman over forty but she carried it off with desperate style.

"You know I always take a house in Carmel for the month of August. Lyle only comes down on weekends," she said airily, dismissing the subject with a languid wave of her hand. "But where on earth have you be hiding? I . . ."

"Uhh, Valerie," Dev interrupted as he turned toward Danielle, who was beginning to feel very much in the way. "You remember Danielle Adams?"

"Mrs. Sheldon."

Valerie Sheldon studied Danielle's face for a moment before her coolly assessing glance slid down her body.

"Oh, yes," she said finally. "Your . . . model. The one who posed for that statue you refused to sell Lyle."

Danielle stiffened defensively and was about to protest when she realized that now she *was* Dev's model—in both senses in which Valerie Sheldon had used the term.

"Miss Adams is not my model," Devlin said without bothering to hide his irritation. "She's the new owner of Valmont's."

Danielle would have been grateful for Dev's quick defense if she could understand why he hadn't bothered to mention that she was also his fiancée. Was he afraid that his *ex*-mistress would make a scene? She was his *ex*-mistress, wasn't she?

"The new owner?" Valerie Sheldon said as if that particular piece of information held as much interest for her as the latest figures on unemployment. She turned her attention back to Devlin. "I've been trying to get in touch with you for weeks. Didn't you get the messages I left with Maggie?"

"No, we haven't been in touch. I've been too busy."

"Anyway, she told me you'd be coming by today and I just had to see you. You're not going to believe what I've got in mind for you." She paused to enjoy her delicious little secret one moment longer, literally licking her perfectly drawn lips in anticipation. "I want to commission a statue from you." As an afterthought, she added, "As an anniversary present for Lyle."

"What kind of statue?" Dev asked with more interest than Danielle would have liked.

"A statue of . . . me." She tossed her blond mane, flashing Devlin a smile that was embarrassingly girlish.

"Just like the one Lyle wanted to buy that wasn't for sale."

"Well, I . . ." Dev started to say before he was interrupted by a high-pitched squeal of delight.

"Hey, there's the man!" Ellen, Maggie Carson's assistant, appeared seemingly from out of nowhere. "Where have you been, stranger?"

"Hi, Ellen." Devlin returned the girl's smile though he could hardly have matched the excitement glowing in her hazel eyes.

"Hi, Mrs. Sheldon," she said, cheerfully ignoring the other woman's withering look to turn to Danielle. "Hello."

"Hello, Ellen." Danielle's smile was genuine. She'd never been more relieved to see anyone in her life. "Is Ms. Carson available?"

"Hey, you know I didn't recognize you at first?" Ellen shook her head in amazement, causing her frizzy halo of hair to wobble, as she took in Danielle's new outfit. "Wow, have you changed. You look great!"

"Thanks, but I . . ."

"Oh, yeah!" she exclaimed as her mind took a sudden turn in another direction. "Maggie told me to keep an eye out for you. She's waiting in her office. She left *me* out here to handle all these people by myself." She sighed dramatically. "Come on, I'll announce you." Heading for the office, she threw a last wistful glance in Dev's direction. "See you later."

Dev grabbed Danielle's arm as she turned to follow Ellen without a word. "You won't be long, will you?"

"I'll make it as fast as I can," she said honestly. She couldn't wait to get out of there.

"How many times would I have to pose?" Danielle heard Valerie Sheldon ask Devlin while she followed Ellen down the hall.

"Poor Dev." Ellen sighed, raising her eyes tragically to heaven. "When that one sinks those platinum-tipped nails into a man, she never lets go."

"Ms. Carson is expecting me, isn't she?" Danielle asked, trying to change the subject.

"Oh, sure, but watch out." Ellen's voice dropped to a conspiratorial whisper. "She's in one of her blue funks today." She sighed tragically again, as though she didn't know how she managed to cope. Stopping in front of the closed office door, she rapped on it twice before opening it just enough to stick her frizzy head in. "Miss Adams is here, Maggie."

The muffled reply came after a moment of silence, "Please send her in."

"Good luck," Ellen mouthed cheerfully before she hurried off to rejoin Devlin, who was deep in conversation with Valerie Sheldon.

Forcing down the old doubts and fears that were beginning to surface, Danielle walked resolutely into Maggie Carson's office. Closing the door behind her, she was struck, as she had been the first time, by the claustrophobic feeling of the room. The framed pictures of Valmont which covered all four walls overwhelmed the already small space and seemed to draw the very oxygen out of the air. She found it difficult to breathe the tobacco-stale air that remained.

Maggie Carson herself seemed somewhat lost between the desk piled high with papers and the large blowups of Valmont's face which surrounded her.

Quickly stubbing out a cigarette, she rose and hurried forward to greet Danielle. "I'm so glad we finally got to meet one another," she said warmly, "even though I've been a bit nervous about it."

Danielle was surprised at her sincerity. "I have too," she said rather lamely.

The two women stared at each other for a moment, trying to match the image they'd created in their minds with the person now standing before them.

Maggie Carson wasn't at all what Danielle had expected in a home-wrecker. Slim and petite, she was in her early fifties, but even as a girl she wouldn't have been considered a beauty because of the unevenness of her features. Yet the spirited intelligence that shone through her dark eyes and animated her strong-boned face, coupled with a generous mouth, made her strikingly attractive. Her skin was unnaturally pale for a native Californian, and though relatively unlined, had that puffy look of someone who drinks too much. Short ash-brown hair, liberally sprinkled with gray, framed her face softly and, except for a touch of lipstick, she wore no makeup. Her black silk tunic dress brought out the dark circles under her eyes and gave her the look of someone in mourning.

"How very lovely you are. How proud Valmont must have been of you," she said, continuing her own inspection. "You have your father's eyes," she added with a sharp little gasp as though it hurt her somehow. "The same . . . incredible deep violet eyes."

"I'm afraid that's where the resemblance ends," Danielle said uncomfortably.

"Oh, no," Maggie disagreed. "You have the same

. . . quality. You even carry yourself the way he did. Proud, withdrawn but with that same . . . magnetism he had that always drew you to him in spite of yourself." Her voice cracked and Danielle realized that Valmont's ex-wife still loved him after all these years.

"Listen to me carrying on," she said, laughing self-consciously. "Please, make yourself comfortable." She waved Danielle over to the leather chair in front of the desk as she make her way back to hers. "Can I get you something? A drink?"

"No, thank you."

"Are you sure?" she insisted before lighting a cigarette. She drew in the smoke hungrily as if she'd been deprived of nicotine for days instead of minutes.

"Thanks, no," Danielle said, sinking into the chair.

"I think I'll have one, just to mark the occasion." Reaching into the bottom desk drawer, she took out a half-empty quart of Scotch and poured a generous amount into the glass next to her, which still held a trace of the amber liquid. "We've got something else to celebrate," she went on excitedly after putting the bottle back and taking several ladylike sips of her drink.

"What is that?" Danielle asked, feeling grateful that Maggie was carrying the conversation, since she was suddenly having trouble putting the words together to tell Valmont's ex-wife about her decision.

"I'm planning a Valmont retrospective. I've been working on it for weeks. You can't imagine how many people in the Monterey area have early Valmonts. And I've also been calling collectors all over the States, so we should end up with a truly representative show." She took another long drag on her cigarette and several more ladylike sips of Scotch.

"Here . . . these are just some of the paintings on loan." Reaching across the desk, she handed Danielle a manila envelope. "I thought we'd run the show for a month," she continued excitedly while Danielle drew out the contents of the envelope.

She looked at snapshots of some of Valmont's earliest and best work, each of which had the owner's name printed neatly on the back, while she listened to Maggie Carson describing her plans in detail.

A successful businesswoman in her own right, Danielle found herself admiring the woman's professional know-how and executive ability. She was clearly an independent, strong-minded woman. Her only weakness, Danielle realized sadly, was her love for Valmont. Her love and appreciation of art were as evident. Danielle was sure now that Maggie Carson had been instrumental in getting Valmont's career started. The situation was becoming increasingly difficult for her.

"I didn't tell you about all this before because it didn't become final until yesterday," she told her when Danielle handed back the envelope. "But I'm very interested in any suggestions you might have." She paused to light another cigarette on the butt of the last one, which she then put out in an ashtray already overflowing with cigarette butts. "I thought we'd have the opening on the twenty-eighth of September. It's going to be a bit tight but, as you know, that's Valmont's birthday. He would have been fifty-five . . . only fifty-five." Her voice broke off and she took a fairly unladylike gulp of her drink.

"Uhh, Ms. Carson," Danielle began.

"Please, call me Maggie," she insisted warmly. "After all, we are both part of Valmont's family . . . in a way."

"In a way" was about the best way to describe it, Danielle thought, but she refrained from saying it. Unlike herself, Maggie Carson obviously still had illusions about Valmont. She watched silently as the woman sought to recapture her earlier excitement.

"You will come to the opening, won't you, Danielle? It's on a Saturday. You can fly in from Boston and stay the weekend."

"But I'm not going back to Boston, Maggie." Danielle took the opening and plunged ahead. "I've decided to stay in Big Sur. That's what I wanted to talk to you about."

"But I thought you said . . . at the end of the summer . . ."

"No, I told you I would give you my decision about the gallery at the end of the summer. And I've decided to . . ." She was unable to go on.

"To take over the gallery," Maggie finished for her. "I see."

Danielle suddenly needed a drink, but she would have settled for a cigarette even though she didn't smoke, just to help her cope with the feelings of guilt that were beginning to swamp her. "I'm sorry, Maggie, but now that the restoration of the house is almost finished, I have to go back to work. I have to make a living too and . . ."

"Oh, I understand." She smiled with obvious difficulty before taking another desperate drag on her cigarette. "Really I do. It just came as a shock since you've never shown any interest in the gallery . . . until today."

Danielle leaned over the edge of the desk. "I would be delighted if you were to stay on here and work with me."

"Oh, no." She shook her head forcefully. "Thanks anyway but . . . I couldn't."

Danielle was about to insist but she realized how difficult it would be for Maggie to work as an employee in an establishment that she'd run for almost twenty years. Danielle was suddenly furious with Valmont. She felt an impulse to pull the drink out of Maggie's hand and smash it to pieces against one of his smiling portraits.

She took several deep, calming breaths instead. "Didn't Valmont leave you anything?"

"Oh, of course. Two of the nudes I posed for," she said with deep gratitude which only infuriated Danielle more. "They're worth quite a lot, especially now that he's . . . I could never sell them, of course." She lit up another cigarette and squashed out the butt.

"I wish you'd reconsider my offer," Danielle said sincerely.

"Do you mind if we talk about the . . . details of the transfer some other time?" she aswered, trying not to appear as upset as she obviously was.

"Of course not." Danielle got to her feet but found herself unable to walk away. "What are you going to do now?"

Maggie exhaled a ragged stream of smoke. "I don't know. I still can't believe that he won't be coming back this time," she replied, though Danielle had been referring to her work. She finished off her drink in one gulp then stared into the empty glass for a moment. "You know . . . Amy, your mother . . . and I were the closest friends . . . until Valmont. I never tried so hard not to love someone."

Danielle was left speechless by the unexpected confession and the realization that she no longer felt any resentment for the woman who had broken up her home. Having also fallen desperately in love in spite of herself, she was finally able to understand Maggie Carson's actions. And she realized that her love for Devlin—like Maggie's for Valmont—would endure long past their inevitable breakup.

"I know what you mean, Maggie," Danielle admitted softly.

"Oh, I hope not . . . for your sake," Maggie said sadly but without self-pity. "Still, given half the chance, I would do it all over again."

"Yes," Danielle agreed, and a tiny shiver of fear went through her. When she looked at Maggie Carson's devastated face, she saw herself years from then. "Please let me know if you need anything," she offered sincerely before she let herself out.

The last things Danielle saw before she closed the office door behind her were the tears glistening on Maggie Carson's face and the shrine she'd created to an impossible love. The last thing she heard was the scraping sound of the bottom desk drawer being pulled open.

10

ooooooooooo

Don't you think we should talk about it, Danielle?"
Devlin asked when, shifting gears, he turned off the
restaurant parking lot onto Highway 1, heading for
home.

From the moment Danielle left Maggie Carson's
office, she'd been depressed. Having to wait a good half
hour for Devlin to disentangle himself from Valerie
Sheldon, only to run a gauntlet of art groupies, hadn't
exactly helped her mood. The drive back to Big Sur had
seemed unusually long and tense.

The Nepenthe restaurant, which Dev had selected for
their celebration dinner was, justifiably, the most famous one in Big Sur. Perched on the very edge of a
cliff, its wall of windows overlooked fifty miles of
dramatic, ocean-sculptured coastline.

They chose to dine outside on the sprawling, multileveled patio where their rough-hewn table looked out over the tops of the trees. It was only inches from where the rock sheered away in a dizzying descent into the Pacific, which thundered and pounded against its ragged edges.

No matter how hard Danielle tried to enjoy the spectacular view and delicious food, she was unable to shake off her depression. Instead of lightening her mood, the champagne she drank only darkened it further. Even Devlin's attempts to cheer her up had failed. They ended up having dessert and coffee in tense silence, watching the dying sun being swallowed up by a blood-red sea.

"We're not in a public place now," Devlin persisted, reminding Danielle of her reason for not explaining her mood at dinner.

"I'm sorry I ruined your evening," she said miserably.

"You didn't. I just wish you wouldn't shut me out when you're upset." He gave her a quick, worried look. "I thought you'd stopped doing that."

"You're right; we have to talk," she admitted with difficulty. "Do you mind if we go back to my place tonight, Dev?"

If he did, he didn't make it apparent, but it took him a moment to murmur his OK.

"You were so happy earlier, that's what I can't understand. Did something happen with Maggie Carson?" he probed when Danielle still hadn't said anything. "I know you were anxious about meeting her. How did it go?"

Feelings of guilt, edged with that nameless fear,

welled up inside her just at the mention of it. "God, it was awful."

"I was afraid she might give you trouble. Is she going to fight the takeover?"

"No. No, she accepted my decision completely but she was . . . terribly upset about it." Maggie Carson's devastated face came back to haunt her. "I never realized the gallery meant so much to her and I . . . I feel just awful about taking it away from her."

"Danielle, it was your *father's* gallery," Dev reminded her emphatically. "He wanted *you* to have it."

"But Maggie's the one who's been running it all these years. She's the one who's responsible for its success . . . not me. And certainly not Valmont." She exhaled a long, harsh breath. "That selfish, insensitive—even dead he's still screwing up other people's lives . . . making them suffer."

"I wouldn't shed too many tears over Maggie Carson, if I were you," Devlin stated flatly, keeping his attention fixed on the dark, winding mountain road which only the car headlights illuminated. "Valmont made a quarter of a million dollar settlement on her when they divorced. Add that to the money she's made from the gallery all these years and . . ."

"Well, if that isn't your typical self-centered artist talking," Danielle lashed out at him angrily. "Ready to buy a woman off when you get tired of her. What about Maggie's feelings? That gallery is her whole life. It's the only life she's ever had, thanks to Valmont. She's still in love with him, for God's sake! Doesn't that mean anything?"

"I know you're angry at Valmont," Devlin said

carefully, gripping the steering wheel with suddenly whitened knuckles. "But why take it out on me?"

"What makes you any different?" she blurted out bitterly.

"What the hell is that supposed to mean?"

"Nothing. Forget it." Danielle turned to stare out the side window.

"Like hell!" Tires screeching, Devlin swung the XJ-S abruptly onto the shoulder of the road and slammed on the brakes. He turned to face her, but for a moment, the only sound in the car was the idling motor. "I want to know what you meant by that, Danielle."

"All right," she agreed coldly. "Look at the way you've treated Valerie Sheldon. It's pretty obvious she's still in love with you but now that you've found someone new, you dropped her without giving a damn about her feelings."

"What are you talking about? I never *dropped* Valerie Sheldon because I never took her up in the first place." Devlin paused to search Danielle's face in that penetrating way of his. "Is *that* what you're so upset about?" he murmured, astonished. "Where did you get this crazy idea about me and Valerie?"

"Are you saying that you weren't having an affair with her when I first met you?"

"That's right. Then or at any other time. I thought you knew me better than that by now," he muttered dryly, shifting automatically into neutral. "Even if I were attracted to her type of woman, which I'm not, I could never have betrayed Lyle's trust. Lyle and I have been friends for years. He was the first collector to take an interest in my work."

"Well, his wife certainly takes an interest in you," she said sarcastically. "Which you don't exactly discourage."

"If I seem to indulge Valerie's crush on me . . . and that's all it is," he explained patiently, turning around in his seat so he could face her, "it's only because I understand that it's the result of sheer panic on her part. She's terrified of getting old and losing her looks. That's the same reason Lyle accepts her meaningless flirtations."

"Is that also the reason you agreed to do a nude statue of her?" Danielle demanded before she could stop herself.

"I did not agree," he protested, impatience beginning to creep into his tone. "You were standing right there when I told her I'd have to think about it."

"*And* when you told her that I was the new owner of Valmont's. What you neglected to tell her was that we're getting married next week!"

"Why should I have told her?"

"Why didn't you?"

"Why didn't you tell your grandmother?"

Danielle was stunned by the hurt she saw in his eyes. She hadn't realized that he'd felt it to be a kind of betrayal, but she couldn't answer him because she didn't know herself why she'd been unable to tell her.

"Damn!" Devlin fell back against the seat with a heavy sigh. "We really do need to talk." Shifting into drive, he released the brakes and swung the car smoothly back onto the road.

"Dev, I . . ."

"Let's wait till we get back to your place, OK?" he said shortly. "Or we'll both end up over a cliff."

They made the rest of the short trip in silence. Devlin concentrated on the narrow, unpredictable road winding along the very edge of the cliff; Danielle stared down at the wild, craggy beauty of the coastline almost a thousand feet below. In the pale glow of the half-moon, the breakers shattered into a million bits, sparkling like wet diamonds on the stranded boulders.

Except for a murmured "thank you" when Devlin helped Danielle out of the car, no words were exchanged as they walked to the front door or as she opened it and led him into the house and down the hall to the living room.

Switching the overhead light on, Danielle continued inside with far more assurance than she was feeling. Devlin paused in the doorway, looking around with a bemused smile. The living room was a mess. Dustcovers shrouded the furniture, giving it a ghost-like appearance, and paint-dotted newspapers covered the floor. All the scatter rugs were rolled up in one corner of the room and a ladder and several empty paint cans occupied another.

"I know it looks a mess. I just finished painting yesterday," Danielle explained self-consciously. "But everything's clean and it is the most comfortable room in the house."

Actually, the most comfortable room in the house was her bedroom, as Dev's smile made irritatingly clear. For obvious reasons, Danielle felt it would be better to talk in here.

"Besides, I thought you might like a drink . . . I know I would," she rattled on, dropping her pocketbook onto the floor next to the sofa. "I'm sure I saw a bottle of brandy when I cleaned out the bar the other day."

"I'll get it," Dev offered, waving her back to the job of removing the dustcover from the Chesterfield couch. "But which one is the bar?"

"That one." Danielle pointed to a shrouded rectangle before she began neatly folding the dustcover. "I think the room will look really nice once it's finished, don't you?" she said, trying to keep everything on a less explosive level than before. It would be difficult enough to tell Devlin her decision, and she was determined to be mature and unemotional about it. She was shaking inside.

Either Devlin didn't hear her or he chose not to answer. While he poured out the two brandies, Danielle carefully wiped the tufted leather couch with its dustcover before she sat down on the edge, neatly crossing her legs at the ankles.

"Danielle, I love you," Dev stated flatly when he handed her one of the crystal snifters and sank heavily down on the couch next to her. "I thought you'd come to believe that during these last two months and to finally trust me. But I see now that you don't." He stared morosely into the amber liquid he was swirling around in his glass. "I've never had an affair with Valerie, and I have no intention of doing a statue of her . . . for several reasons, but that's not the point." He looked up at her with deeply troubled eyes. "What bothers me is that you seem to think that if she were to pose for me I would automatically go to bed with her. Am I right?"

"Well, she is a . . . very beautiful woman," Danielle admitted with difficulty. "And in such an . . . intimate situation any man would be tempted to . . ." Unable to deal with the pain that thought caused her, she took a shaky gulp of her brandy.

"I told you before, the studio is where I work. My work often includes nude models but when I look at them, it's as a sculptor, not as a man." Sensing that he wasn't getting through to her, Dev shook his head in frustration and took a long, hard swallow of brandy before he tried again. "As an artist, when I look at a naked woman, all I see is a series of problems that have to be solved before I can capture that life in stone or clay." He leaned toward her. "Can you understand that?"

Danielle fell back against the couch, annoyed that the nearness of him affected her so deeply. "Are you saying that you've never had an affair with any of your models?"

"No, I didn't say that. I've gone out with several of the women who've posed for me over the years," he admitted unashamedly. "I've even gone to bed with some of them but never in the studio when we were working." He smiled wryly. "That the artist always sleeps with his models is another one of those myths people love hearing about."

"Valmont was always sleeping with his models," she countered archly.

"I am not Valmont!" Angry frustration brought him to his feet. "I could never take advantage of the situation for one thing . . . and I wouldn't get much work done either."

"You *didn't* get much work done the time I posed for you," she reminded him.

"That's not fair . . . not even for you," he said bitterly. Slamming his brandy glass down on the shrouded cocktail table in front of the couch, Dev stalked over to the fireplace as though he needed to put some distance between them in order not to lose his temper.

"What happened between us," he went on in a tightly controlled voice, "happened only because of the way we feel about each other, not because you were naked. And the women who come to the studio to pose for me are professional models who are there only to do a job . . . and a damn difficult one at that." He took a step toward her, the effort to control himself tautening every muscle of his powerful body as he added caustically, "No professional model would have reacted the way you did."

Danielle gasped soundlessly as what happened that day suddenly came alive between them, flooding her mind with unforgettable images. Once again, she saw his strong, sensitive fingers molding the statue in her likeness. The exquisitely tender way his thumb moved over the rounded curve of a hip and glided with long, sensuous strokes along the soft undercurve of a breast, making her own breasts tingle, her nipples harden with excitement. But the thought that he could do that to someone else ripped through the beautiful memory, cut through her like a knife. "Valerie Sheldon isn't a professional model."

"And Valerie Sheldon has nothing to do with what's going on here either!" Devlin finally exploded. "You're just using her as an excuse! What do you really want, Danielle?" He strode back to the couch and stood there towering over her. "Do you want me to get so mad at you that I'll walk out . . . like the last time? Is that what you want?" Bending down, he grabbed her roughly by the shoulders, pulling her up off the couch. The brandy glass slid out of her hand and shattered on the floor. "Well, I'm not going to walk out! So you might as well tell me what's really bothering you!"

"You're right. Valerie isn't the problem," Danielle cried miserably. "It's *us!* Our life-styles are too different . . . that's why it'll never work out between us. And that's why it's better to break it off now before . . ." Twisting out of his grasp, she staggered back several steps, too upset to care about the glass splintering under her heels. "Because no matter how much I love you, I'm not going to end up like Maggie Carson! I can't . . . I won't build my whole life around someone only to have it destroyed when you get tired of me and move on to your next . . . inspiration!"

"What are you talking about?" Dev threw his hands up in an almost supplicating gesture. "I'm not looking for a short-term affair. I want to marry you."

"Maggie Carson was married," Danielle said with a kind of defeated anger. "So were Valmont's three other wives." Kneeling down, she quickly rolled up the shards of glass in some paint-splattered newspaper and stashed the bundle under the cocktail table with trembling hands.

Devlin watched her wordlessly, a bitter smile twisting his mouth, until she got to her feet again. "I've been expecting this," he muttered. "Signing that marriage license today really scared the hell out of you, didn't it? I knew you'd find some excuse to call off the wedding because *you're* the one who's afraid to make a lifelong commitment—not me."

"No, I'm not," she protested, tears stinging her eyes. "If only I could believe it would be a lifelong commitment."

"I can't make you believe it, Danielle." Dev shook his head sadly. "Belief is something that can only come from inside you, and you're too afraid to even try." He took a step toward her and she noticed a sudden softening in his tense features, in the depths of his amber eyes. "I know how difficult it is for you. Everyone you've ever loved has abandoned you one way or another . . . Valmont, your husband, even your mother. But you can't let that . . ." —

"It's not that!" She turned to walk away from him, from the soft pleading in his eyes and voice that was rapidly weakening her resolve. He snagged her wrist, pulling her back to him.

"When are you going to stop running away from yourself?" he demanded angrily. "Your real self, the one you discovered here in Big Sur with me?" He released her wrist only to grab her bare shoulders. "What are you going to do now? Go back to Boston . . . and Howard?" His fingers dug painfully into her flesh as if he wanted to hurt her as much as that thought hurt him. "Or are you going to run away to another city . . . another man?"

"No, of course not," she cried angrily. His words hurt her far more than the painful grip she was struggling to break free of.

"Because no matter where you go, you're never going to find anything better than what we've got," he vowed fiercely. "You couldn't go back to what you were before even if you wanted to. You're too alive for that safe, empty life your grandmother and Howard have all mapped out for you. You've got too much to give to . . ."

"Oh, my God," Danielle gasped as she went limp under his hands."

"What?"

"That's exactly what Valmont said to me the last time we met."

"I thought you told me he put you down," Devlin muttered, releasing his grip on her. "Because he was disappointed in the way you'd turned out."

"That's what I thought," she murmured distractedly. "Well, he criticized my job and Howard and . . . he said I was becoming like the rest of my mother's family." A wry smile twisted the corner of her mouth in spite of herself. " 'The living dead,' he called them."

"Maybe he was trying to tell you that you were too alive for the life you were leading . . . too much woman for the man you'd chosen," Devlin suggested quietly. "But wasn't that the reason you left Boston to come to Big Sur?"

"He did say I was throwing myself away on a man like Howard," Danielle admitted while managing to evade Dev's question.

She paused as that last, traumatic meeting with

Valmont slowly unreeled in her mind. Except for a lingering feeling of rejection, she'd blocked it out completely, until that moment. She viewed it now with a strange kind of detachment, as though it were a scene in a movie, and she was able to see it objectively for the first time.

"I remember now," she said falteringly, like someone struggling to read the subtitles of a foreign film. "He said that he wished he could help me meet a man who was worthy of me . . . but there wasn't much of a chance unless . . . unless he could find some way to get me away from my grandmother's influence."

"Now we know why he left you the studio," Devlin said pointedly. "And it sounds to me as though he felt that he'd let *you* down. I told you he must have loved you, in his own . . . imperfect way."

"If only I'd understood what he was trying to tell me, instead of acting like a defensive little snob," Danielle said regretfully, sinking down on the couch. "I didn't know he had only a few months to live, but I'm sure now that *he* knew. That's why he came to see me so unexpectedly." She pressed her clenched fists against her stomach, which was beginning to hurt. "And we parted on such bad terms. I didn't even cry when he died."

Danielle burst into tears. Covering her face with her hands, she jumped up blindly from the couch but Devlin blocked her with his body.

"No, don't run away from me," he pleaded. Taking her in his arms, he pulled her back down on the couch with him.

Instead of helping her to get herself back under

control, the warm, comforting feel of his arms broke what little resistance she had left. Burying her face in his chest, Danielle gave in to the deep, racking sobs which shook her, letting herself feel the love for her father which she'd denied all her life. It felt as though the pain of a lifetime were pouring out of her, as though her tears were dissolving the wall she'd built around herself, washing away all her guilt and fears.

Devlin had been the only one able to penetrate that wall and she clung to him now, overwhelmed by the intensity of the emotions ripping through her. She felt sure that if Dev's arms hadn't been there to hold her, she would have come apart. He held her in his arms until she cried herself out.

11

~~~~~~~~~~~~~~~

For a moment, Danielle wasn't sure what it was that first broke through to her consciousness—that warm weight pinning her leg to the mattress or that funny, tickling sensation making her nose itch. Wiry little squiggles danced before her barely focused eyes and got tangled in her lashes. It wasn't until she dragged her reluctant head up from its firm cushion of flesh that she recognized Dev's chest hair.

With boneless fingers, she scratched the tip of her nose as reality came back to her in blurry pieces: the sensation of her softly rounded body melting into the hard smoothness of his; the slow, steady, hypnotic rise and fall of his breathing; the intoxicating warmth of their mingling body heat. Along with the awareness of her surroundings came the memory of Devlin carrying her, still sobbing, into the bedroom last night, his getting into bed with her when she begged him to stay, the tender way he had held her in his arms until she fell into an emotionally drained sleep.

He was still holding her, though he was lying on his back now, a possessive arm clutching her to him while she snuggled up against his side, an arm and a leg half-sprawled across him. It still amazed her how perfectly they fit one another. Missing the feel of him, her head fell back softly onto his shoulder, sending her hair spilling over it in thick, shiny black waves.

Without waking, Dev shifted slightly, fitting her head snugly into the muscled curve his arm made around her shoulders. Her leg was all pins and needles. The powerful leg he'd slung over it some time during the night tautened when she attempted to carefully slide hers out, as if reluctant to let go of her. Anchoring her leg even more firmly to the space between his, Dev unconsciously pressed the vulnerable inside part of her thigh against the outline of his dormant sex.

Danielle thought she felt him beginning to stir, but because of the pins and needles in her leg, and the fabric barriers of her nightgown and his jockey shorts, she wasn't sure.

"Yes, my love," he murmured in his sleep with a sexy little growl, hugging her closer. "Oh . . . yes."

Now there was no mistaking a definite prodding, like tentative little knocks against her own stirring flesh. A sigh that was her name escaped him and his hand released her shoulder to glide searchingly down her back over the swell of her hip. He smiled softly, sensuously, as his body remembered hers in his sleep, letting her invade his dream.

A rush of love went through Danielle. She'd never felt so open. The tears she'd shed had dissolved all her defenses, emptying her of the doubts and fears that had always come between them. Her love for Devlin filled all the emptiness. She knew now that it always would.

With an almost physical longing, Danielle contemplated Dev's face in the tremulous light of a dawn which streaked across the sky in shifting, melting pastels. Spilling through the windows, it turned the white plaster walls the color of mother-of-pearl and softly burnished his copper skin. In sleep, Dev's strong, craggy face was as trusting as a child's.

Unable to keep from touching him any longer, even if it meant waking him up, she reached out to trace the lines of his face with soft, lingering caresses. Mingling her name with a sigh again, Devlin sank his fingers into the rounded curve of her bottom and unerringly found her breast, with his other hand. Danielle suppressed the laugh bubbling up inside her, in spite of her own growing passion, as the love taps on the inside of her thigh grew more insistent. Smoothing his sleep-rumpled hair, she retraced his face with tender little kisses.

His lips parted, reaching blindly for hers, even as his consciousness struggled up through the daze of sleep to find her. Smoky topaz eyes fluttered open under his tawny lashes, then glowed with recognition mixed with surprise. "I thought it was just . . . a dream," he murmured with a warm, sleepy smile that went right through her, melting her utterly.

"No, it's not a dream," she breathed, bringing her trembling mouth down on his.

Dev's reaction was instantaneous and total. She would never have believed that anyone could wake up so fast. Wrapping both arms around her, he pulled her effortlessly on top of him, deepening the kiss as he took control of it. Danielle's mouth opened under the delicious assault of his, welcoming the possessive thrust of his tongue. Winding her fingers in the tangled mass of his hair, she clung to him, giving herself up mindlessly to the erotic sensations only he could arouse in her.

But that wasn't what she'd wanted!

"No . . . wait," she cried breathlessly when she was able to drag her mouth away. "Wait!" She managed to push away from him and pull herself up on her knees, straddling his strong, hard thighs. The sheet that had been covering them slid off, falling in a soft heap at the foot of the bed. Her breath caught in her throat at the sight of his body, naked except for jockey shorts, gleaming in the iridescent light of dawn. She wondered if she would ever get used to how beautiful he was.

She felt the sudden tension in his hands, which were still gripping her shoulders, and noticed the change in the depths of his eyes, a kind of pulling back. "I just want to show you how much I love you," she reassured him, a funny little catch in her voice. Reaching up, she took his wrists in her trembling hands. They were so large, her fingers barely closed around them. "I just want to love you . . . the way you love me."

Devlin's relieved surprise made it easy for Danielle

to slide his hands off her shoulders, though he couldn't have been more surprised at her daring than she was.

"Let me," she pleaded softly as if she were somehow afraid that he might try to stop her, but she didn't wait for his answer. She'd waited long enough to prove the depth of her love for him. Forcing his arms gently down on the pillow, she stretched them out on either side of his head, her fingers entwining with his. "Let me love you?"

Dev's answer was a sharp intake of breath. His fingers tightened around hers almost painfully when her tongue darted out to trace and retrace the outline of his lips. Finally, easing past them, it slid inside to taste the sweet, moist warmth of him, to search out and torment the most sensitive areas in a way she'd learned only too well from him.

Reverting instinctively to the dominant role, Dev sought to catch and hold her bottom lip with his teeth but Danielle slipped out of his reach to trail burning little kisses the length of his arched throat. For an endless moment, she let the wildly beating pulse at its base throb under her parted lips. It reverberated deep inside her, sending ever-widening circles of love and longing through her.

Moving down, she buried her face in the damp, tawny curls on his chest. There was a small indentation there and her chin fit perfectly into it. She pressed her trembling lips to the spot, breathing in the unique musky scent of him. Aching for the feel of him, her fingers slid out of his, gliding down his arms, to caress his torso softly, slowly, one delicious inch at a time.

"What are you doing to me?" he gasped, his legs

shifting restlessly under her. The effort it cost him not to reach out and grab her tautened every muscle of his body.

"I'm not doing anything to you that you don't do to me," she reminded him with a breathless little laugh, her eyes glowing at her own daring. But she wanted to give him more, to give him back all the love he'd ever given her.

Her hands continued tracing sensuous patterns all over his heated flesh. They moved with long, urgent strokes from his shoulders to his hips as though trying to touch all of him at one time. The skin on her palms had become extremely sensitive and she was amazed at the erotic sensations touching him aroused in her as well. When her mouth moved down his body to retrace those patterns with hungry little kisses, she found that she was shaking as much as he was. She couldn't get enough of him. And Dev's intense reactions to her loving, the way he gave himself up to her totally, urged her on to still more daring expressions of her love for him.

A shudder went through him and his muscles coiled convulsively under her. "That's not . . . fair," he protested thickly. "I want to feel you too." No longer able to restrain themselves, his hands reached out to tangle impatiently in the folds of her nightgown.

Sitting back up on her heels, Danielle allowed him to pull the delicate, lacy covering off her body with one motion and throw it clear across the room. But when he reached out to try and capture her breasts, she pushed his hands away. They fell back onto the pillow with a soft thud.

"Here, my love," she whispered raggedly, "feel me too." Bending over again, she brushed her full breasts over his chest with a caressing motion, gasping as the wiry curls scraped her swollen nipples. Dev moaned deep in his throat and his nails bit into the palms of his hands as they clenched into fists.

Danielle moved down the long, taut length of his body slowly, tantalizingly. She barely heard the strange little sound she made—half-laugh, half-moan—when she felt the hard, insistent love taps against her naked breasts. Curling her fingers into the elasticized band of his jockey shorts, she tugged them off him clumsily. Her hands were shaking with excitement but she managed to slide them off one leg only to leave them dangling from his other ankle. The beauty of him held her transfixed. Reaching out, she touched the tip of him softly, almost fearfully, before tracing the warm, velvety hardness.

"Yes, touch me!" Arching his hips with a strangled moan, he pushed into her hands and she took all of him. Danielle gasped with a kind of awe at the life-giving power throbbing in her hands. It stirred something deep inside her—an ache, an emptiness longing to be filled. Her hair spilled all over his chest when she bent her head to kiss him, tentatively at first, and then deeply.

A groan tore from Dev's throat and his hands grabbed violently onto the head posts, making the four-poster shudder beneath them.

The pleasure she gave him, which transfigured his face and shook his body, filled Danielle with a strange, joyful power. It was a purely female sense of power that she'd never experienced before, would never have believed herself capable of, and she gave herself up to it completely.

Lifting herself over his body, she took him deep inside her, surrounding him utterly. His sharp cry at the impact of their coming together echoed hers, and her body contracted just as violently as his, her knees digging into his sides. Waves of pulsating heat washed over her as she moved on him, sweeping her farther and farther away from herself, tossing her finally like driftwood onto the safe, hard shore of his body where she clung wildly.

"Kiss me!" Dev urged fiercely, bringing his burning mouth up to hers. Powerful arms locked around her, crushing her against him as if he meant to dissolve the barrier of flesh that separated them. Mouths and bodies, hardness and softness all fused together, making them one.

Danielle held nothing back. Until that moment she hadn't realized that she'd always kept a part of herself locked safely away. Now, with both of them poised on the shattering edge of ecstasy, she dared to give Devlin all of herself, denying him nothing, taking him deeper and deeper, taking him with her, beyond everything.

She felt as if her skin were a shell that had disintegrated. Her heart fluttering wildly inside her, she clung to him in the hazy aftermath, tears of joy misting her eyes. Like a butterfly burst free of its chrysalis, she felt all new. Reborn.

Epilogue

~~~~~~~~~~~~~~~~

Sorry I'm late," Danielle called out to Devlin as she slid out of his wedding present—a fire-engine red Alfa Romeo.

Devlin must have been listening for her return because he had the front door open before she turned off the ignition. He looked every bit the eager new husband of less than a month as he hurried over to her. Having driven at the speed limit all the way back from Carmel to get home to him, Danielle rushed into his arms just as eagerly.

"I missed you," he murmured with a little growl when he lifted his lips from hers. His arm went around her shoulders, hugging her to his side.

"Me too." She buried her face in the hollow of his neck, the tangy warmth of his skin. He dropped a kiss on top of her damp hair. Only then did he notice the light rain streaming down on them.

"Come inside," he urged.

Still clinging to one another, they ran through the rain to the open doorway, laughing like children. The door closed securely, Dev moved to kiss Danielle again, running his hands down her back. He released her abruptly. "You're all wet."

"It was pouring in Carmel. I've been getting rained on all day." Danielle laughed again but a tiny shiver of cold went through her.

"Come on over to the fire." Devlin helped her out of her damp jacket. "I've got just the thing to warm you up."

"I'll bet you have," she teased.

"I knew there was a reason why I missed you. I just didn't know what it was." Dev's golden eyes reflected happiness tinged with humor as he and Danielle made their way over to the sunken living room. "So how did it go? You didn't have any problems, did you?"

"Oh, no. The lawyer was already waiting in Maggie's office when I got there. All I had to do was sign the necessary papers for the transfer. But Maggie insisted on opening a bottle of champagne afterward to celebrate."

"I would think so," Devlin muttered wryly. Propelling her directly in front of the blazing fire, he bent over to grab a couple of pillows off one of the love seats. "I'm sure she never expected such generosity on your part."

"It wasn't generous . . . just fair. And I think Valmont

would have approved." She plopped down on the pillow Dev had tossed onto the Navajo rug in front of the fireplace. "Besides, I don't need the gallery . . . not now that I'm opening my own. 'Ours,'" she amended with a smile, since she intended "The Wilders," which would specialize in sculpture, to be a showcase for Devlin's work. "I took Maggie over to see the space; that's why I'm late," she added when Dev sank down onto the pillow next to hers. "She had some terrific suggestions. She even offered to help me put the first show together. With her experience and established clientele, I don't see how we can miss."

"Just as long as you're happy. That's all I care about," Dev said earnestly before he reached for the glass mugs warming on the hearthstone in front of the fire. "Here . . ." He offered her one of the mugs of mulled wine that he'd fixed while he was waiting for her. "This should warm you up . . . before I finish the job."

Wrapping her chilled hands around the steaming mug, Danielle murmured half-jokingly. "You're going to spoil me."

"I'm trying."

"You're succeeding," she assured him softly. "You've already spoiled me for any other man." She smiled tremulously. She still wasn't used to so much happiness. Suddenly, she didn't need the artificial warmth of the drink. All she wanted was the very real warmth of Dev's mouth and body. Turning to put the glass mug safely out of reach on the cocktail table in back of them, Danielle noticed the statue resting on it for the first time.

"Oh, Dev! Is this the new piece you've been working on so hard? The one you wouldn't show me until it was finished?"

"Uhh . . . yes." His voice held an uncharacteristic trace of insecurity. It touched her that her opinion meant so much to him.

Danielle contemplated the foot-high, expressionistic clay study, which was still attached to its armature. It took her a moment to make out the figures of a man and a woman sitting side by side because the flowing lines of their hair, arms, and body melted completely into one another. Like all of Dev's work, the emotional and sensual impact was stunning. But when Danielle realized that the chubby form sprawling across their laps, literally growing out of the loving merger of their bodies, was an infant, she burst out laughing.

"What's so . . . funny?" Devlin tensed visibly beside her. "Don't you . . . like it?"

"Oh, yes, it's beautiful!" she assured him but amusement lingered in the depths of her violet eyes when she turned to look at him. "It's just that . . . are you sure you're really a sculptor, and not a sorcerer?"

"What?"

"Well, you know how sorcerers always made clay figures to work their enchantments on? I just realized, that's what you do."

"Me?" He couldn't have looked more confused. "How?"

"First you made a statue of your fantasy woman . . . and we met because of it. Then when I was trying like hell to resist you, you created a statue of lovers, and before it was even finished *we* became lovers. And now . . . this." She smiled at him, unaware that her loving smile was exactly like that of the female figure. "I could be wrong but *this* . . ." she added wryly, indicating the sprawling infant, "looks like another Wilder enchantment to me."

"I didn't realize my fantasies were showing." Devlin grinned that tentative, totally disarming grin of his. "Would you mind that very much?"

"Oh, no. There's nothing I could possibly want more." Just the thought of it made Danielle's throat tighten. She had never allowed herself to believe that such happiness would ever be hers. Running her fingertips impulsively over the chubby, amazingly alive-looking form of the baby, she suddenly realized that *her* deepest fantasy had always been to be part of a family. Something she'd never known. "Dev, we can't sell this. It's the most beautiful thing you've ever done."

"It just might turn out to be my masterpiece." He chuckled. "However . . ." Setting his glass mug down on the cocktail table, he took her in his arms. "This is one masterpiece I can't create without your help."

Danielle wound her arms around his strong neck, pressing her breasts softly against his chest. "You know I'll pose for you."

"Actually, I had a different kind of help in mind." Firelight flickered in the golden depths of his eyes as they searched hers deeply. "And a different kind of creation," he whispered raggedly on her mouth, pulling her urgently down onto the pillows with him.

Danielle's lips parted under his, and she went all open to him, giving herself up completely to the enchantment of Devlin's lovemaking.

The smile on the face of the female figure seemed to take on a Mona Lisa quality as it gazed down at the artists in the joyous act of creation.

YOU'LL BE SWEPT AWAY WITH SILHOUETTE DESIRE

$1.95 each

11 ☐ James	37 ☐ James	63 ☐ Dee	89 ☐ Ross
12 ☐ Palmer	38 ☐ Douglass	64 ☐ Milan	90 ☐ Roszel
13 ☐ Wallace	39 ☐ Monet	65 ☐ Allison	91 ☐ Browning
14 ☐ Valley	40 ☐ Mallory	66 ☐ Langtry	92 ☐ Carey
15 ☐ Vernon	41 ☐ St. Claire	67 ☐ James	93 ☐ Berk
16 ☐ Major	42 ☐ Stewart	68 ☐ Browning	94 ☐ Robbins
17 ☐ Simms	43 ☐ Simms	69 ☐ Carey	95 ☐ Summers
18 ☐ Ross	44 ☐ West	70 ☐ Victor	96 ☐ Milan
19 ☐ James	45 ☐ Clay	71 ☐ Joyce	97 ☐ James
20 ☐ Allison	46 ☐ Chance	72 ☐ Hart	98 ☐ Joyce
21 ☐ Baker	47 ☐ Michelle	73 ☐ St. Clair	99 ☐ Major
22 ☐ Durant	48 ☐ Powers	74 ☐ Douglass	100 ☐ Howard
23 ☐ Sunshine	49 ☐ James	75 ☐ McKenna	101 ☐ Morgan
24 ☐ Baxter	50 ☐ Palmer	76 ☐ Michelle	102 ☐ Palmer
25 ☐ James	51 ☐ Lind	77 ☐ Lowell	103 ☐ James
26 ☐ Palmer	52 ☐ Morgan	78 ☐ Barber	104 ☐ Chase
27 ☐ Conrad	53 ☐ Joyce	79 ☐ Simms	105 ☐ Blair
28 ☐ Lovan	54 ☐ Fulford	80 ☐ Palmer	106 ☐ Michelle
29 ☐ Michelle	55 ☐ James	81 ☐ Kennedy	107 ☐ Chance
30 ☐ Lind	56 ☐ Douglass	82 ☐ Clay	108 ☐ Gladstone
31 ☐ James	57 ☐ Michelle	83 ☐ Chance	109 ☐ Simms
32 ☐ Clay	58 ☐ Mallory	84 ☐ Powers	110 ☐ Palmer
33 ☐ Powers	59 ☐ Powers	85 ☐ James	111 ☐ Browning
34 ☐ Milan	60 ☐ Dennis	86 ☐ Malek	112 ☐ Nicole
35 ☐ Major	61 ☐ Simms	87 ☐ Michelle	113 ☐ Cresswell

Silhouette Desire

$1.95 each

115 ☐ James	134 ☐ McKenna	153 ☐ Milan	172 ☐ Stuart
116 ☐ Joyce	135 ☐ Charlton	154 ☐ Berk	173 ☐ Lee
117 ☐ Powers	136 ☐ Martel	155 ☐ Ross	174 ☐ Caimi
118 ☐ Milan	137 ☐ Ross	156 ☐ Corbett	
119 ☐ John	138 ☐ Chase	157 ☐ Palmer	
120 ☐ Clay	139 ☐ St. Claire	158 ☐ Cameron	
121 ☐ Browning	140 ☐ Joyce	159 ☐ St. George	
122 ☐ Trent	141 ☐ Morgan	160 ☐ McIntyre	
123 ☐ Paige	142 ☐ Nicole	161 ☐ Nicole	
124 ☐ St. George	143 ☐ Allison	162 ☐ Horton	
125 ☐ Caimi	144 ☐ Evans	163 ☐ James	
126 ☐ Carey	145 ☐ James	164 ☐ Gordon	
127 ☐ James	146 ☐ Knight	165 ☐ McKenna	
128 ☐ Michelle	147 ☐ Scott	166 ☐ Fitzgerald	
129 ☐ Bishop	148 ☐ Powers	167 ☐ Evans	
130 ☐ Blair	149 ☐ Galt	168 ☐ Joyce	
131 ☐ Larson	150 ☐ Simms	169 ☐ Browning	
132 ☐ McCoy	151 ☐ Major	170 ☐ Michelle	
133 ☐ Monet	152 ☐ Michelle	171 ☐ Ross	

SILHOUETTE DESIRE, Department SD/6
1230 Avenue of the Americas
New York, NY 10020

Please send me the books I have checked above. I am enclosing $_____
(please add 75¢ to cover postage and handling. NYS and NYC residents please
add appropriate sales tax). Send check or money order—no cash or C.O.D.'s
please. Allow six weeks for delivery.

NAME_____

ADDRESS_____

CITY_____ STATE/ZIP_____

Silhouette Desire